Arrogant Billionaire's Do-Over

An Enemies to Lovers Surprise Pregnancy Romance

Ivy Karr

Copyright © 2023 by Ivy Karr

All rights reserved.

No portion of this book may be reproduced in any form without written permission from the publisher or author, except as permitted by U.S. copyright law.

Contents

1. Chapter 1 — 1
2. Chapter 2 — 12
3. Chapter 3 — 24
4. Chapter 4 — 35
5. Chapter 5 — 46
6. Chapter 6 — 57
7. Chapter 7 — 72
8. Chapter 8 — 82
9. Chapter 9 — 97
10. Chapter 10 — 113
11. Chapter 11 — 121
12. Chapter 12 — 136
13. Chapter 13 — 149
14. Chapter 14 — 157
15. Chapter 15 — 166

16.	Chapter 16	174
17.	Chapter 17	183
18.	Chapter 18	193
19.	Chapter 19	201
20.	Chapter 20	212
21.	Chapter 21	220
22.	Chapter 22	229
23.	Chapter 23	236
24.	Chapter 24	244
25.	Chapter 25	251
26.	Chapter 26	259
Epilogue		267
Also By		270
Also By		271
Also By		272
Also By		273

Chapter 1

The Scandal

Kevin

"Sandra Henry has walked out of her wedding!"

I switch channels.

"Actress and model Sandra Henry opens up about her affair with billionaire playboy Kevin Wills."

I switch the channel again.

"Forty-year-old, billionaire playboy Kevin Wills, the owner of Wills Entertainment Agency, has been involved in a scandal," The announcer reads, 'Sandra Henry, a critically acclaimed model and actress, finally speaks up after....'

"This is bullshit!" I yell as I throw the remote at the television screen. However, the annoying, high-pitched paparazzi can still be heard through the speakers, spouting lies.

Well.... Half-truths, but lies all the same.

First, Sandra and I had stopped dating almost a year ago, and she was about to get married to someone she met after we broke up.

Why am I the one receiving all the attention?

"Sir, I just got off the phone with the PR team; they'll see what they can do to get you out of this," James says as he walks into my living room, tapping away on his phone.

As he puts the phone down, he notices the broken TV screen and sighs. He brings the phone to his ear and says apologetically, "Hello? Marcus? I'd like to order another TV. Do you have anything that doesn't break?"

I suck my teeth in frustration and make my way to the wine bar, pouring myself a shot of whiskey, "It's so stupid! Why do they twist the story? Don't they have anything better to write about?"

"We're still going through the texts between you and Sandra, but we will get you out of this scandal," He assures me.

James Daniel is thirty-four years old and has been my assistant for four years. He's been a good partner and knows many things about me, including what I like and what I don't like.

If he says he will fix something, he'll fix it. A wonderful ally. But this is his first time fixing something as stupid as this.

The reporters aren't entirely lying. I enjoy good things - wine, money, and women, with more emphasis on the latter.

I met Sandra through work. She started as a model a few years ago, and I hired her because of her talents. She had no problem getting both modeling and acting jobs, and she quickly became one of my agency's top talents, with producers battling and outbidding each other to get her on their sets.

We bonded adequately on a few dates here and there, and then we started going steady. It was an extremely confidential relationship, and only my assistant was aware of our relationship. We broke up because I got bored. Being tied down to one woman hasn't really been my thing.

Now, she turned down her fiance and claimed to still be in love with me. With the secret of our former relationship out, the other actresses and actors in my agency are now convinced that I favored her because I was in a relationship with her.

I've been clear from scandals throughout my career, but this is the first time something like this has happened, and the media have been in a frenzy. I've not even been able to set foot into my own office. I was glad my residence has remained private, but who knows when the media would sniff it out to get here?

I need to get away from here.

"Sir, you need to leave," James suggests.

I'm focused on my drink, so I am still determining where he's looking. I turn to find him staring out the window through the blinds with a frown on his face.

"What is it?" I ask as I join him by the window and take a look. Sure enough, they've found my residence, "Those little mosquitoes."

"We need to get you away from here, at least until things settle down," James suggests, "Out of the country would do."

"No, I can't leave," I say with an exasperated sigh, "I still have to watch over my company and this whole mess. I need to go somewhere I can lay low in the US."

"What about one of your properties in Malibu? You can enjoy both Santa Monica mountains and the Pacific Ocean at this time of the year," he says, trying to lighten the tension.

"Hmm... make it Malibu," I say, "One of my properties is in the hills. Extremely private. Get the plane ready."

"Will do, sir," he says, preparing to make the call.

It's about time I take a vacation, also. Away from New York and all this madness. Once this matter gets resolved, I don't see myself spending more time with any woman for a long time.

The hilly terrains in Malibu. The area isn't treacherous or steep, and it still makes the perfect spot to escape the madness in New York.

I actually need the break.

Most talent agencies flock to Hollywood to make the best out of the thriving talents. But I set up my base in New York and basically monopolized the market there.

While starting the agency with less competition was easier, finding the projects for my talents became more difficult.

I remember the time when I would beg producers to hire my talents for support roles or extras. Sometimes, I would ask the local companies to hire our talents for their ads or hire my upcoming artists to perform gigs at events people had never heard of.

It is exhausting, mentally and physically. With James by my side, I started taking it easier. The only moments I had to myself involved trysts with beautiful women. Then again, it involved getting them to work for me too.

No, I didn't manipulate them. They all had different intentions but were committed to their roles and dedicated to work. Still, with Sandra's case making waves now, I've come to the conclusion that it's time I kick back and relax.

I will commit to her and start a family if I ever find the ideal woman.

"Is that all you think about? Your career? I have a career too, Kevin," she said with a broken voice. "Don't you think that it's high time you think about not being a playboy and actually being a man?"

All of a sudden, the words of a woman from the past returned to me.

It's been years since I remembered anything she ever told me.

I have also started forgetting what she looks like.

But why am I choosing to remember her now?

I shake off the thoughts and focus on the road.

I needed privacy, so I didn't come with my driver. It's been a while since I drove myself. I left all of my cars back in New York, but James rented a luxury sedan for my stay in California.

Arriving at the property at the top of the hill, I step out of the car and admire the house built out of wood and stone: only five bedrooms and a pool to dip in. Well, it looks like the pool could use some cleaning.

It's not the most significant property I own, but I love the privacy it offers while still being not too far from the crowd.

The caretaker of this property checks on this house once a month, but due to my sudden unplanned visit, he did not have a chance to prep the place before I arrived.

ARROGANT BILLIONAIRE'S DO-OVER

I enter the house and stare at the furniture covered in cloth to prevent dust from settling on them. The white fabric looks a bit darker from the settled dust.

I haven't been to this property in two years, so I hope the caretaker of this property checked on the integrity of the appliances and maintained them properly.

Also, because it has been a long time since I've been here, I don't have any of the house staff to take care of things. I don't know any cleaning companies in Malibu either.

I pull out my phone and dial James.

"Did you arrive safely, sir?" He asks as soon as he answers the phone.

"I just arrived. Do you know any cleaning companies in Malibu?" I ask as I run my fingers across the cloth.

"I forgot you wouldn't have any house staff over there," he replies, "I don't know any cleaning companies in your area, but I will look for one. I do know a good catering company. Are you hungry?"

"Famished," I reply, then I look around the house. It is smaller than my other places, and I have nothing to do. James will handle most of the responsibilities in the office, and all I need to do is check-in, review, and respond to the reports James prepares for me.

"Never mind the cleaning company. I'll be bored out of my mind," I sigh, "I'll handle the cleaning myself."

"I didn't know you were able to clean," he teased, "Thanks to you, some cleaning workers in New York can send their children to college."

I don't know why he finds ways to insert his humor, but it always helps me relax.

"Very funny," I roll my eyes, although he can't see me, "About the catering service, I want to keep it simple as too many cooks can spoil the broth."

Besides, having too many people coming over here to cook would be problematic, considering I'm trying to hide my presence here.

"I understand, sir. No worries. At this catering service, you can request only one chef, and they have NDAs and so on," he explains, "I'll hire their best chef exclusively for you."

"I'd like that. Have the chef come over soon," I say to him, waiting for his confirmation from the catering service, before hanging up and turning my attention back to the living room.

After placing my things in the bedroom, I get to work immediately, making sure the entire building is rid of dust and other items that would make it unsightly to others. Who knew I could be this homey?

I'm done cleaning.

I had to remove my shirt and switch into shorts to simplify cleaning, but now I'm sweaty.

I take in a deep breath and exhale the same.

It's uncomfortable with the sweat on my body. Still, as I look around, I'm actually impressed with myself and how much work I have put into the house.

It's been ages since I've done my own cleaning, so it's still bizarre.

The plan was to use the opportunity to forget about everything that was going on right now.

It worked because I hadn't considered anything besides keeping my sanctuary clean.

"All right then," I say softly.

But as I speak, it's almost like there's an echo. There's no one else here.

Usually, I would have a guest, so I wasn't alone. But I can't afford to have anyone over.

Probably, the chef James is trying to hire won't be the kind of person who wants to sit down and share a glass of wine with me.

"Maybe I should check if there are any women to pick up around here. Oh God... Have you learned anything, Kevin?"

I accept the internal reflection of my thoughts and make my way to the kitchen for a cold glass of water.

As I pour myself the glass, I look out the window and just take in the view.

I know I'm not supposed to think about what's happening in New York, but there's just so much I can do to pretend nothing's happening.

"Maybe I don't want to be just another fling. Maybe I want to get married and start a family someday. Don't you want to relax and enjoy conversations at one of your properties while we take in the view together and I cook you one of the best meals you've ever had?"

Her voice. My heart starts to ache a little.

It's been a long time since I've actually thought of her. But the recent backlash made me regret a lot of things I have done.

Most of the women I had brief relationships with eventually got married or committed to a long-term relationship.

Even some colleagues of mine are settling down. James says he's planning on taking the next step with his girlfriend next year.

Maybe... maybe I was wrong about not taking the relationships more seriously...

There's a knock on the door, followed by the sound of a doorbell.

My phone chimes at the same time, and I get a message from James, saying my chef is on her way.

Not to sound misogynistic, but I was expecting a male chef only because I'm still conscious of women in my life.

I make my way to the door. I don't bother putting on a shirt because I'm already too sweaty.

The doorbell goes off again.

"I'm coming, I'm coming," I grumble as I open the door.

The fresh air makes contact with my skin, cooling me off.

No... it's not the air. It's her.

I don't usually believe anything is coincidental, but I have been thinking about her. Unconsciously, of course.

Her words, *"Is that all you think about? Your career? I have a career, too, Kevin. Don't you think that it's high time you think about not being a playboy and actually being a man?"*

To think that she's back again in my life.

And as my chef, no less.

Chapter 2

Who Is At The Door?

Lydia

"Mommy, I want chocolate," Alex says in a melodic plea.

There's no better feeling for me than being a mother to this adorable creature.

His beautiful eyes, little pointy ears and nose, and chubby little cheeks that are currently being puffed because I'm ignoring his plea are enough to make my heart thump a little faster.

"You had chocolate yesterday," I say to him as I squeeze his cheek a little.

"Only a little," he looks like he's on the verge of crying if I don't give him what he wants.

"Fine, after you come home from the daycare today," I promise him.

"Can I have some on my way there?" He insists as he hugs me, squeezing harder for extra effect.

I can't keep being his pushover, but I can't help myself.

I let out a sigh, reaching for the jar I've kept out of his reach, and hand him two small chocolate bars.

"You aren't having any more chocolate. Do you hear me, young man?" I warn.

"Yes, mama," he says in a sweet tone, but the mischievous look in his eyes tells me that he will probably use the same strategy again.

Just as it has always worked, again and again.

But I don't mind it.

Life as a single mother can be challenging, but just knowing my little boy is there to make every day worth working a little harder is all I need to keep me going.

I drop off my little ray of sunshine at the daycare.

"I wish other kids were a little more like Alex," Mariam, one of the daycare teachers, says to me as we both watch Alex try to calm down a child refusing to let her mom go.

"I'm sure they are all unique in their own ways," I say to her, but it's just a facade to hide how much pride I have when it comes to my baby.

"They all are, and I'm glad parents like you trust us to take care of them," she says with a warm smile, "Have a great day at work today. Will you be early today?"

"I'm not sure, but if I'm not here, my sister will pick him up," I reply.

"Oh, Lily," she calls my sister's name.

"Yes, that's my sister. All right, have a great day, Mariam."

"You too," she says and bids me farewell.

I turn around to look at my baby, and he's already calmed down the girl. They hold hands and make their way to the building.

I give a satisfactory nod and head to the office.

Malibu is the city of superstars and the like.

I'm twenty-eight years old, and thanks to my job as a chef for a catering service company, I've been able to meet with different celebrities or society's VIPs.

It's been a wonderful experience.

As someone who loves to cook, I get to do what I love and provide for myself and my son without any struggles or dependency on anybody for support.

ARROGANT BILLIONAIRE'S DO-OVER

I've spent the last six years perfecting and working on my craft, improving my skills, and expanding my achievements. Now, I'm the top chef at Peak Bites, Malibu's biggest and most successful catering service.

People go out of their way to book my sessions or services. Yes, there's envy from other chefs and cooks, but you can't be jealous of someone who has actually put in work.

As I make my way through the halls and down to the kitchen, I can feel the eyes on me. Most are staring out of admiration.

"Look, it's Chef Lydia Johnson."

"I heard she was asked to serve the mayor."

"Did you know she won the Emerging Chef award?"

"Such a strong woman dedicated to her work."

I keep my head high but stay humble and keep learning. I don't want the past achievements to get to my head and stop growing.

The arrogant will fall in ways they do not expect.

But I'm afraid compliments are not the only thing I'm getting from my colleagues.

"There she is again. She thinks she's all that."

"I hear she got in here through a favor."

"Do you think she's actually good? She probably steals recipes from other chefs."

"She's already a single mom. I guess her baby daddy couldn't stand her at all."

Human beings are fickle when it comes to their own sense of pride. But I don't let that bother me either.

There are tons of things they could bother themselves about. For instance, they can improve their craft rather than just cautiously spilling words they deem fit, forgetting the wind carries their whispers to their targets.

I ignore them.

Who cares if I'm all that?

What if I *did* get in here through a favor?

Steal recipes? We're chefs, and most of the food we make has been made by thousands, if not millions, before us.

And marriage? Who needs that?

Some men have shown me that wanting a proper family is the last thing on their minds. Instead, they would rather run around going after different women or chicken out of becoming parents when their partners become pregnant.

Who cares if Alex doesn't have a father figure? I'm enough of a parent for him.

Allison is the first to notice me as I open the kitchen doors.

"There's my number one chef!" She announces as she makes her way to me with open arms.

I open mine as well to prepare for her embrace. As she hugs me, a wave of relief washes over me.

Alison started working here five years ago. Unlike the others who spend time judging me, Allison is among the chefs who want to learn from me.

She's the one I was most comfortable working with. Alex also liked her, so that was a plus.

"How is the number two chef doing?" I ask.

"You mean the future number one chef," she corrects me, winking. "You don't know this, but you're actually an old woman. And I'll soon take the number one title right under your nose."

"You're older than me... thirty-three, " I remind her with a raised brow.

"Shhh... I don't want these kids to find out," she says as she looks around to make sure no one is straining their ears to listen.

I look around as well.

The others will always look for something to gossip about during breaks, and I'm genuinely getting tired of being a subject.

"Oh, by the way, did you hear? Sandra Henry walked out of her wedding!" She says.

"Allison, you know I have no interest in showbiz gossip," I roll my eyes as I get ready to get to work.

The office was also a restaurant. I don't have kitchen duty today, but it's not so bad to help out in the kitchen once in a while.

"You should be interested," she says with a frown, "these people are your future clients. You should at least know what happens in their personal lives. To know who to avoid and such."

"The only thing I should be interested in is what kind of food they like and what they're allergic to," I point out, "I can't forget the time I fed a client some shellfish and later found out she was allergic."

"Didn't she tell you to prepare whatever?"

"She did at first, but she told me about her allergy when I presented the meal," I explain, "Then again, I guess it's my fault as I didn't even ask her what foods are a major no or yes."

"Pfft. Don't come crying to me for any celebrity advice," she says with a scoff as she gets to work as well.

"Lydia? A minute, please," the boss calls to my attention.

His office has every award Peak Bites has ever received, along with his own achievements. There's not a single photo of him here, though.

What is the thought process behind his actions? I have no idea.

"You wanted to see me, sir?" I ask.

"Yes, we have a very special order," he replies, "someone will be needing your services for a month. He goes by James Daniel and wants you to take care of his boss, who stays in the hills."

I've had orders like this before, but usually for a few days or a week.

It will be the first time I've ever had to work for an entire month for one person. It's a breakthrough of the year.

"That sounds very nice," I say with a smile, "Am I starting right away?"

"Yes. And it's an unusual case," my boss says, leaning forward on his chair and intertwining his fingers. The expression on his face turns serious, "The client wants you to be very discreet about his identity and doesn't want anyone to know about his address. He's even willing to pay double for you."

"Double?" I ask in disbelief.

"Yes. We'll be paying you the extra money and take our percentage from the original price," he explains.

"Thank you so much, sir," I say to him.

"It's All right. You're a hard worker and brought us a lot of opportunities. You're not our top chef for no reason," he says, "Even some of my customers ask for you instead."

I don't know how to respond to that statement, so I keep silent and just nod.

"All right, gear up and leave once you're ready," he orders, "Get ingredients that will serve for breakfast, lunch, and dinner. He doesn't have anything there, and we'll also be handling his groceries."

It might sound like I'm complaining, but this client is probably going to treat me like his maid or something.

"I can't help but feel like you're going there to be a maid of some sort," he says, almost like he's reading my mind.

"I'll be fine, sir," I assure him.

"All right. Take care," he says, "The client has already paid in advance. So I'll send it across."

"Thank you," I say, "Oh, did the client mention any allergies?"

After completing my shopping list, which consisted of different ingredients to cook and a complimentary fruit basket, I made my way to the client's house.

The area is very much secluded, and I can't help wondering what kind of client he would be.

Luck has been on my side, and I have never gotten any client that has made my job difficult. My colleagues would complain about so many clients who treated them poorly, so anytime I meet a new client, I can't help but worry.

But judging by the generosity of this mystery man, I may be in luck yet again.

I make my way to the front door, too distracted by my nervousness to take in the beauty and simplicity of the place.

After knocking on the door and pushing the doorbell,

I hear footsteps approach the door.

"I'm coming, I'm coming," the voice on the other side says.

As soon as I hear the voice, my heart sinks into a panic.

It can't be.

It shouldn't be.

Anybody but him.

The door opens, and I find him again. As soon as he set his eyes on me, his shoulders dropped as well. And he looks at me like he's seen a ghost.

"I'm at the wrong house," I say and turn to leave.

"Lydia?" He calls, stopping me in my tracks.

His voice is as rough and gentle as it used to be. There's something else mixed with it. He seems more mature, but I don't care and honestly don't want to.

"Are you the chef from Peak Bites?" He asks.

I take in a deep breath and turn around to face him. I placed a mask of uninterest, switching to a professional smile.

"Chef Lydia Johnson, top chef at Peak Bites, at your service," I say, acting like everything is okay.

"I..." he stops, at a loss of words.

My eyes lower, and I notice he's shirtless. The glistening on his chiseled abs and broad chest suggests he worked up a sweat from some kind of physical activity before I arrived.

"May I come in?" I ask, forcing my eyes away from his body and looking up at his face.

"Sure," he frowns and goes into the house, leaving the door open for me.

I bring the groceries in and close the door behind me.

"I got you the groceries, and I'm aware that you have no allergies. I made sure that everything I purchased would be healthy for you," I explain, then pick up the basket and hand it over to him. "I also brought you a complimentary fruit basket, courtesy of our management. I hope you enjoy it."

He accepts the basket, exchanging glances between me and the gift. His face suggests many questions are running through his mind, while mine shows I'm not interested in answering any of them.

"How would you like to be served? I can make a limited number of dishes but enough to satisfy your palate," I continue the script I'm required to repeat to every client.

"Why are you talking like that? Don't you remember me?" he asks.

"Sir, I would like us to keep this professional," I reply, shutting him down, "Anything else would be unethical."

The frown on his face deepens, and I can see a vein at the side of his forehead. After all these years, it's still very easy to get him pissed off.

But still.

This is going to be the most awkward client I'm going to work with.

Chapter 3

Blow To My Pride

Kevin

Eight Years Ago

When I first saw her, I had already begun making a name for myself – primarily among small businesses that relied on me to create advertisements.

I enjoyed popularity and financial success, rolling in my millions. It was during this time that I first felt drawn to the influence women held.

There was a certain allure in having women admire you.

I mean, why wouldn't they? At that time, I was a young, handsome millionaire running a business in New York, a venture that many would leave for Hollywood to pursue.

I found myself fending off advances many times. None resisted me.

However, life doesn't always unfold perfectly.

I visited Chicago frequently for my business, and one day, I met her at a small diner not too far from my penthouse in Chicago. I was hungry, and it was the only place around to get food fast, so I went in.

"Welcome, sir. We'll get you seated and take your order shortly," she greeted with a warm smile.

It felt odd. I assumed that many customers had already seen that smile countless times. As a talent agency owner, part of my job involves encountering individuals who frequently smile at me. Yet, it seemed like her smile was genuinely directed at me.

I couldn't look away.

She was short, 5' 4", a petite frame. Her face was rounded, which made her seem a little childish; her eyes were genuine, but there was a hint of mischief in them.

Her lips and dark reddish brown hair complemented every aspect of her beauty.

I was stunned.

"Sir?" She called, "Is everything All right?"

"You're stunning," was my reply.

"Thank you," she said in response, and it broke my heart.

The way she didn't falter, unaffected by what I said, told me that she had heard the compliments so many times that they no longer had any effect or power over her.

It was frustrating, but there was nothing I could do about it.

"Just tell me what you would like, and I'll have it ready," she said with a smile.

"I will eat anything you make," I smirked.

"Nice try, mister," she said as she placed her arms at her side, "I cook the meals here, so you might be in luck."

"All right then, I'll have burgers," I placed my order.

She nodded and left for the kitchen, leaving me to stare at her swaying hips as she left for the kitchen.

A strange feeling stirred within me.

I wanted her.

I found myself visiting that restaurant again and again.

Everything she made tasted so good and increased my desire for her.

We finally got to spend time together outside her work hours, and she shared her dreams and hopes with me, telling me about everything she hoped to achieve before she turned thirty.

Opening a restaurant of her own was the main goal, with others including working at a top restaurant or even buying a house with a beautiful kitchen made for a chef.

I could have easily gotten everything she wanted with my connections, but she didn't ask for my help. No..., it was evident that she never needed my help.

We started dating, or at least that's what she thought.

Personally, I felt it was too early to settle down. I believed there was much more to experience, and the idea of being tied down meant potentially missing out on other opportunities to be with different women. Reflecting on it now, I realize it was a shallow perspective, and I'm ashamed that I once thought that way.

"What is your plan for us?" She finally asked, three months into our relationship.

It was a peculiar situation—we hadn't engaged in sex, but we'd shared numerous passionate moments. We were together in my penthouse in Chicago when she popped the question that night.

"Plan? What do you mean?" I asked.

Her shoulders dropped, and I immediately knew I'd failed to respond to her question correctly.

"You don't know what I mean?" She asked, "We've been together for three months now, and I just want to know where this is going."

I didn't say anything, hoping she would change the direction of this conversation.

"You know, I actually thought we were in a relationship at first," she confessed. "But lately, I've started to feel like I am the only one who sees it that way."

"I never said we were steady," I reminded her, "And besides, we can't be in a relationship."

"Why?" She asked, and I watched her hands ball into a fist.

"Well, I mean…" I struggled to find the words. It was an unusual experience for me as I'd never had a problem finding words to express my thoughts before that moment.

Her eyes bore into me without saying a single word.

"I have to think about my career," I offered the most ridiculous excuse, "I don't want the negative public reviews. Besides, the whole Playboy thing helps with the marketability, you know? So I…."

I stopped talking.

The hurt in her eyes cut deeper than any knife ever could.

"Is that all you think about? Your career? I have a career too, Kevin," she said with a broken voice, "Don't you think that it's high time you think about not being a playboy and actually being a man?"

"Wait, calm down," I said, "We can still be lovers, though. Like maybe we…"

"Maybe I don't want to be just another fling. Maybe I want to get married and start a family someday. Don't you want to relax and enjoy conversations at one of your properties while we take in the view together and I cook you one of the best meals you've ever had?"

She stood up and reached for her purse.

"What are you doing?" I asked.

"Something any sane woman with a shred of self-respect would do," she replied in a cold tone.

I'd never seen her that way, and she'd never looked at me like that before.

I felt ashamed.

"Wait, let's talk it out," I pleaded.

"I'm not that easy. Empty words won't dissuade me. Maybe I let you trick me into believing you before, but not anymore. Never again," she said it with every fiber of her being, and I could tell she meant it.

"If you want to be like that, then leave," I said as I rolled my eyes.

"Fine," she replied and left without slamming the door.

I was left alone, and for the first time in my life, I realized something significant that I had often overlooked to maintain a sense of well-being.

I was, in fact, an empty man.

It's been three days since she started working at my house.

She arrives as early as seven thirty to prepare my breakfast, sticks around and makes me light snacks, makes lunch, and then excuses herself.

She returns around five, gets dinner ready, and leaves.

She barely talks to me unless it's related to the meals she's making for the day or asking my preference.

I hate it. It's annoying when she acts like she has never met me before. I find it really frustrating.

But does it bother her? Not even in the slightest.

I can't let myself be humiliated for the second time, and this time, I'm going to remind her what she used to be attached to.

Seven thirty a.m.

The sound of the doorbell announces her arrival. I make my way to the door and open it with a smile.

She's dressed in a knee-length skirt and long-sleeved shirt. Her hair has been tied into a ponytail. She's gotten a little curvier, and her baby face has matured a little bit.

There's no time to think about all that. It's time to get my game on.

"You look lovely today," I say with a smile.

I just woke up a few minutes ago, so I still have my morning deep voice.

"I rather not, sir," she says, rejecting my compliment.

"It's just a compliment," I say, trying to stay in character.

"I don't need it, sir," she says a little more sternly, "Let's keep things professional."

"Stop calling me *sir*," I insist as I walk away from the door, gesturing for her to come in.

"All right, Kevin," she finally calls me by name.

"I still don't understand why you have to act like a stranger," I sigh. "We know each other. Yes, the years might have passed, but you don't have to act like you don't want to be here. You can just leave if you want to."

"I don't think you've noticed, but I genuinely don't want to be here," she says, making me a cup of coffee, "I'm still here because of three reasons. One, you've already paid double. Two, I'm representing the company I work for. I don't want to ruin the Peak Bites' reputation. Three, the other chefs are all booked, and I can't switch with anybody else. I'm afraid I'm stuck with you and not the other way around."

This woman!

After she's laid down her reasons, I'm too stunned actually to say any words. It's obvious she sees me as nothing more than a nuisance.

"Besides, you just can't stop flirting with any woman who comes near you," she says sarcastically. "I heard about your little fiasco with Sandra Henry. She walked out of her wedding because of her undying and unyielding love for you." She chuckles, "To think someone loved you enough to walk out of her wedding with another man. I guess she wasn't the only one who thought life together with you was possible."

"To think someone loved you enough to walk out of her wedding..."

She didn't have to add the last statement. It's totally unfair.

Does she expect me to apologize for what happened years ago? Not me! Never!

"Do you need any help?" I ask, trying to change the topic.

"What's with the scowl? Did I touch a nerve?" She smirked.

"No. Not at all," I lie.

She chuckles and continues to inspect the ingredients she's brought for today.

"I guess I could use a little help," she says with a sigh, not even lifting her head.

Usually, every woman swoons as soon as she makes eye contact with me. It gives me a kick, knowing that it's easy to make them desire me.

But Lydia…

"Make sure you chop the vegetables properly," she instructs and comes next to me. She holds my hands and corrects my pace. "Smaller pieces," she says.

I miss being with her like this.

She didn't see me as a billionaire.

She was happy for my advances but focused more on achieving her dreams.

While most people would treat me like a god or would go out of their way to impress me, she didn't seem to care about any of that.

Strange... Why is my heart at peace and in turmoil at the same time?

As I help her make Eggs Benedict for my breakfast, I'm surprised that I'm preparing the meal with her, following her instructions. The last time we were together, I just left her in the kitchen.

But now, every moment I spend with her excites me. It's not normal. Something is happening to me, and I don't like it. I feel like I am losing control.

Didn't I promise myself not to get involved with any woman?

And this is Lydia we're talking about. She walked out of my life because I didn't want anything to do with marriage. She cut off any communication with me and ignored me for years.

It's true. I didn't even bother to ask for her forgiveness because I didn't care.

"You make a good chef," she says as she plates the meal, "You're actually quite pleasant when you follow my instructions."

"Don't push it," I sigh, then take a look at the meal we both spent time creating.

"What's the matter?" She asks, tilting her head with a curious look on her face.

"I'm just amazed," I say to her.

She distances herself from me immediately after she's done preparing a meal and serving it. She's now standing a few feet away from the dining table.

Today, I'm going to close that distance.

I walk up to her, and she appears unfazed. I hold her chin and lift it slightly higher. "You've really improved your craft," I praise her, "You've done a fantastic job."

"Thank you, *sir*," she says, holding my hand and taking it away from her face.

Another blow to my pride. This isn't funny anymore.

Chapter 4

Something Changed

Lydia

I let out an exhausted sigh.

"That is your fourth sigh," my younger sister, Lily, says.

We share similar appearances, except she's much taller, hitting 5' 9", while I'm 5' 4". People often mistake Lily as the older sister, but I don't mind.

After another exhausting day of caring for the arrogant man, Kevin Wills, I need her guidance.

I know I'm not supposed to tell anyone else, but she knows how to keep secrets.

"Do you remember Kevin Wills?" I ask.

"The playboy billionaire that you self-hypnotized into thinking you two were an official couple?" She asks.

"Thank you for the kind reminder of my shameful past," I say with another sigh.

"Mommy, I finished this," Alex says, proudly showing me his coloring book. He colored a monkey red.

"It's wonderful, you little Picasso," I praise him with a kiss on his forehead.

He smiles and waddles away with the coloring book.

"Why did you suddenly bring up your ex?" Lily asks, bringing us back to the topic.

"I got a job that I have to work exclusively for this client for an entire month," I explain, "Upon arriving at the destination, lo and behold, it turns out to be Kevin himself."

"Is it such a bad thing?" She asks.

"It wasn't such a bad thing, but I haven't seen him in what, seven or eight years," I explain, "I see him again, and he's barely changed."

"Hmm... What's he doing out here in Malibu? He is from New York, and you guys met in Chicago during his business trip, right?"

"I have no clue why he is here," I reply.

"Maybe he found out about where you work and came here to torment you specifically," she teases.

"Oh, come on," I roll my eyes, "With the amount of pride and the number of women this man had affairs with, I doubt if he came out of his way to see one girl who walked out of his life many years ago."

"True. How has it been? What is it like working for him?"

I pause to think about it. I must say he's been acting differently. The arrogance is still there, but at the same time, his pride gets damaged too easily with each word I say to him.

"It's been strange," I say since that's the only way I can think of summarizing everything that has happened so far.

"Are you... are you thinking of giving him another chance?" She asks with a look of worry in her eyes.

"What? No! Not at all," I shake my head for extra emphasis.

"All right then. Is he the client that paid double the price?"

"Yeah."

"Then you should keep it brief, just work and get out," she advises.

"You don't have to tell me twice," I smirk.

She nods and gets up to leave, "All right, I'll pick Alex up after school."

"Thank you. I'll let Mariam at the daycare know you're picking up Alex," I say.

"Sounds good. See you later, sis," she smiles and waves as she drives away with Alex.

It's not going to be easy working for the arrogant playboy...

"You wouldn't believe this. Remember that time I was trying to tell you about Sandra Henry?" Allison asks.

I had to stop at the office to give updates to my boss and get some more fruits for His Royal Highness.

"Yeah?" I reply.

"It turns out that the man she claimed to be in love with was Kevin Wills, the owner of that popular talent agency," she explains.

"Is that so?" I ask.

"Oh, come on, you really need to put more effort into showing your interest in what I'm saying," she says as her shoulders drop.

"I actually know about this news," I explain.

"What? And you didn't tell me? You cheater," she whines.

It's not like I found out on purpose. It was entirely accidental.

When I learned Kevin was my client. I did some research on the internet and realized that he had continued his playboy lifestyle. Then, I saw the article about why Sandra Henry walked out of her wedding.

I didn't know if I was to laugh or feel bad for him.

"That aside, who's this client you've been working for that have you taken away for an entire month?" She asks.

"You know I can't tell you. I signed an NDA," I cross my arms.

"Oh, come on, please don't be like that," she pleads, "You know I have no one to talk to here."

As if on cue, I start hearing the whispers in the background.

"Aren't they the top two chefs?"

"I bet they wished their roles were reversed."

I send them a nasty glare, and they cringe, retreating like cowards.

Allison is smiling. But it's a pained smile. Allison is married, but she's been having trouble conceiving for five years now. Then there's me with a kid but not married.

It's amazing how people can't resist gossiping and fail to know when to mind their own business.

"Ignore them, Allison," I say to her as I cradle her face in my hands.

"I'm trying, Lord knows," she replies. "But they're just saying that out of spite and jealousy, so I'm not actually that bothered."

A terrible liar.

As my only ally in this building, I can't have her feeling down. I look around, and there's no one paying attention to us. I lean close to her ear and whisper, "The client I'm taking care of is actually Kevin Wills."

Her eyes widen with surprise, and she covers her mouth.

She whispers back, "He's hiding here in Malibu?"

I nod.

"This is hot stuff," she says, "Even if you're only saying it to make me feel better."

She actually believes me, but it's her way of acting like she doesn't know if I'm telling her the truth.

"I bet you're enjoying yourself, getting to feed and take care of a bad boy all by yourself," she says.

"You have no idea. It's not as fantastic as you think it is," I correct her fantasy, "He's arrogant and thinks everyone will just casually obey his command as he wills it. Pun intended."

"Nice one," she chuckles softly. "Well, you're our best chef. You can handle him with no problems."

Now, I've been encouraged by two of my favorite people.

I can handle this.

I arrive at his house, and after ringing the doorbell, he answers the door and waves me into the house.

The malice in his eyes has finally left.

I was getting tired of seeing his frowning face every time he saw me.

Anyway, he's shirtless and has a cleaning cloth in his hand.

He didn't even bother greeting me.

"Good morning, Kevin," I take the initiative.

"Good morning," he replies, sounding a little grumpy, but at least it's not as hostile as it used to be.

I notice him wiping down the TV using a spray cleaner.

The vacuum cleaner is by one of the armchairs, along with some other cleaning materials.

It's been five days since I started working here, but it's my first time seeing him clean the house.

In fact, back in Chicago, I never saw him clean his penthouse because it was done by the cleaning company he hired.

"Why are you cleaning?" I can't help asking.

He pauses from cleaning and looks at me with a raised brow, "Because the place is dusty?"

"I understand that much," I roll my eyes, "I meant to ask why are *you* doing it? If you want, I can recommend you to a company that handles cleaning inexpensively but with quality."

"Did you think a billionaire needs to shop around for an inexpensive cleaning service?" He asks with an amused expression.

"The price doesn't matter. If they're more affordable and can do their job perfectly, providing you with a clean house, then they're worth more," I explain, "Bragging on how expensive your cleaning service isn't really a show-off."

That might have come across as a little harsh. I bet he would give me an angry look next. I brace myself and try to come up with various counterattacks for his angry replies.

"You're actually right," he chuckles softly.

What the heck?

"Normally, I'll jump on the offer to get a cleaning company to handle everything, but I'm actually satisfied doing it myself," he says, "it's been therapeutic for me."

What the hell? Why is he acting so different?

It's not just that. I also noticed that his arrogance isn't as intense as it used to be. He pays attention while I cook, but when I dated him years ago, he ignored me in the kitchen and waited until I was done.

Although he seems a bit irritated whenever we're cooking, I have hardly heard him complain, which is strange.

"Wow, that's pretty surprising to hear you say that," I say.

"What's this?" He raises a brow, tugging a smirk at the corner of his face, "Am I finally making your heart skip a beat?"

"You wish,'" I frown and make my way to the kitchen to get started on his breakfast.

I hear his laughter, but he doesn't follow after me.

I frown.

I let my guard down, and he wasted no time in taking control. But he's going to have to try harder than that if he thinks he can get through to me.

"Ah!" I shriek in surprise as something pokes me in my sides.

I look up, and I find him staring me down; the grin on his face annoys me.

"What was that screech?" He asks while trying to suppress the urge to laugh.

He's too close.

The smell of sweat from his body isn't helping me either.

He places his left hand on my hips, "Are you okay?"

I swipe his hands away and put some distance between us, but it still feels like his hand is on me. It reminds me of when he held me tight and kissed me, making my heart pound out of control.

"Are you okay?" He asks again.

"Don't sneak up on me like that," I warn him, "What if I was holding a knife? I don't want the reputation as the chef who stabbed her clients."

"Understood," he says, looking at the table, "Ooh, toast. Would you like to join me? I'm not that hungry, so I may not be able to finish the meal by myself. If you want, I can make more."

What is this? Did he change his pattern of attack? Am I about to fall for his trap or something?

"I get that you're cautious when it comes to me, but can you at least be open to the idea that I changed?" The frustration in his voice is subtle, and there's a little bit of hurt in it, too.

"No, it's just…. It's still a lot to comprehend," I say softly.

"Okay," he says, gets seated, and starts with a toast, handing me the other slice.

Seriously, what happened to him? Am I responsible for his change in behavior? Did I succeed in making him feel bad? If so, why don't I feel good?

As he takes a bite out of the omelette I made, I watch his face melt into pleasure.

The feeling of pride I get when I see anyone eat my meals is indescribable.

I eat the meal in silence, watching him enjoy it, and I find myself getting comfortable.

"You're still ticklish," he says, trying to break the ice.

"I'm just sensitive, and I wasn't prepared for you to sneak up on me like that," I quickly defend.

"Nice defense," he smiles, "I'm sorry about my attitude when you first came here."

"I apologize, also. But I still think we should keep our interactions at a professional level," I insist.

I don't want what happened in the past to repeat itself. If it ever happens again, I might just lose it.

But I can't tell him any of that.

"I'll try my best," he says with a smirk.

Chapter 5

She Is A Mom Now

Lydia

We've made our truce.

"Thank you for doing a wonderful job, James," he says to his phone.

He's been on a call for some hours and hasn't even touched any of his meals, so I need to heat them up again.

"All right, I'll leave the rest to you," he says as he drops the call.

"Sorry about that," he apologizes as he makes his way to the dining table, "What's for lunch?"

"I made Chinese fried rice," I reply, "I switched up the recipes a bit, but I'm sure you'd like it."

"Oh, where is it?" He asks.

I point at the stove, and I see him frown.

"Don't you frown at me," I cross my arms, "I'm not the one who spent hours on the phone."

"It was work-related," he says, "You could have just left it out, and I'd have eaten it."

"Then you'd leave a review saying I left you cold food," I scoff, "Think again."

He rolls his eyes and sits down, muttering to himself, "All right, what am I supposed to do now?"

I toss an apple at him, and he catches it easily, "I don't want an apple."

"Eat it," I order him.

He stares at the apple and then looks at me.

The frown on his face makes him look childish, and I must admit he does look a little adorable. But not nearly as cute as my Alex.

"Eat the apple. Kevin," I point at the apple in his hand.

"Fine, fine," he agrees and takes a bite, "You're too strict these days."

"Well, as a mother, I have to be strict, or else he'd get away with whatever he wants," I reply.

I'm still the same person who gave in and let Alex have two chocolate bars the other day. I can't let Kevin find that out...

"What did you just say?" Kevin asks, breaking my thoughts.

"What?" I look up.

"You just said, 'As a mother,'" he says with his eyes wide open. I can tell he's in a state of disbelief.

"Yeah, I did," I reply, "I'm a mother."

The apple drops from his hand, and the look on his face amuses me. He's still in complete shock.

"What?" He asks again.

"Kevin, I have a four-year-old son," I repeat myself.

"How?" He asks.

"You see when a man and a woman are together in a room alone..."

"I know how babies are made," he says, then looks at my hands. I know what he's looking for.

"I'm not married. I'm a single mom," I answer his question.

The confusion on his face tells me that he's not sure if he should be happy or worried.

"You've become easy to read these days," I say to him, "Is it part of showbiz? To communicate what you're feeling with your facial expression without speaking?"

"Maybe," he replies and picks up the apple.

The fried rice on the stove is hot and steaming, and I go to retrieve his lunch.

As I plate the hot meal and set it in front of him, he hesitates to start asking.

"Fine, you can ask me," I sigh.

"How did it happen?" He asks.

"It's not something I enjoy talking about, though," I reply as I get seated as well.

"If you're uncomfortable, you don't have to talk about it," he says and starts to eat the meal, but he does not break eye contact with me.

"All right, think of it as a lunch and a show," I tell him.

He nods and adjusts himself while I start my story.

It wasn't long after we broke up. I spent my time working at the diner in Chicago but looking out for opportunities elsewhere.

It was around that time I met him. He's younger than you but a year older than I am.

Maybe it was because I was still nursing a broken heart. I kept my distance from him as long as I could, but he stayed around. He was nicer. Friendlier.

He was a bit too docile for my liking. But all in all, he was really nice to me.

I told him about my dreams. He told me he'd support me, and he did.

I heard about Peak Bites from him, and I tried as hard as I could to get in, but I didn't get a job at first.

Thanks to his encouragement, I was able to get into a proper culinary school. I trained and became the best student at the school in Chicago.

After that, I finally got a job as a chef at Peak Bites, and he moved to California with me. I thought if he were this supportive when I was trying to pursue my career, he would be a perfect partner for me, and I could open my heart to him.

We started talking about getting married and other plans for the future. We couldn't agree on the number of kids we would have because I wanted five, and he wanted only one.

"Five?" Kevin interrupts, then stares at me from top to bottom and repeats, "*Five?*"

"Hush, I love kids. So the more the merrier," I reply to him. "Don't you love kids?"

"I'm an only child, and most of my cousins are the same age or older, so I don't really have experience taking care of children," he answers as he takes a forkful of the fried rice. He's halfway done with the meal already. He must have been really hungry.

"So you've never had a baby fever?" I asked.

"Sometimes, but don't let anyone know I said that," he warns, "Continue your story."

Where was I?

Anyway, things were going well.

My career as a chef took off within the first year of my joining Peak Bites.

Then I got pregnant.

We were worried because it was not our plan to start a family yet. I was worried it could affect my work, but I still wanted to keep the baby.

I explained to him that having the baby together didn't mean we had to get married immediately, and we could just wait and figure things out.

But he started to change.

Well, he wasn't the only one that started to change. When the signs of pregnancy started to show, my colleagues started treating me differently.

I can still remember the whispers of condemnation: Calling me a slut and talking about how easy I was. It was humiliating and frustrating, and I didn't want them to keep getting away with their words.

So I talked to him. Not like I was asking him to marry me, but I just wanted words of encouragement.

Do you want to guess what he said?

"No..."

He said, "I don't think I want to be part of this anymore. I'm not sure I'm ready to be a father. I'm still trying to build my career."

Sounds familiar?

Kevin looks away, pushing his plate aside and letting out a huge sigh.

"I'm just teasing you," I roll my eyes, "But yeah. That's what my ex said."

Then, he stopped talking to me, and soon enough, my messages no longer reached him. Until I stopped seeing him completely. I wasn't friends with anyone he knew, so I couldn't look for him. He was gone, and I was left to take care of myself and the growing baby inside.

"I learned something from both of you, though." I pause.

"What's that?" Kevin tilts his head.

"To build my career." I smile.

I was about to become a single mother, and I knew I needed to be financially stable to take care of myself and my baby, so I worked harder and harder, rising up the ranks and making a name for myself among clients.

Then I gave birth to the most beautiful child I have ever seen. Luckily for me, every single one of his features was a mirror image of mine and none of his father's.

It was not easy, but I became the top chef at Peak Bites, and the money I make is more than enough to support Alex and me.

"So, that's about it," I shrug as I stretch my body, "The story was shorter than I thought it would be."

He's quiet. His eyes are focused on the empty plate on the table. His thoughts are in disarray.

"You must think it's ironic. After everything I said to you in the past, I concluded that I actually don't want marriage," I sit down with a sigh.

"I don't think it's ironic in the slightest," he says, "I'm just feeling bad that this happened to you."

"It wasn't totally a bad thing," I correct him, "I mean, I became the best because it served as a push."

"It's been hard, hasn't it?" He asks.

I stop talking as I notice he's making eye contact. It feels like he's reading all my emotions that I'm trying to keep hidden.

"I don't know what you're..." I try to act tough.

He places his hand on my left. How many years has it been since I felt his touch? His hand dwarfs my hand.

"It's been hard, hasn't it?" He repeats the question, "You've spent years trying to get to the top. I'm sure you've found your way around now, but I'm sure you struggled at the beginning, didn't you?"

I did.

Kevin continues to read me like an open book, "I'm sure you acted tough when they said those words, but I bet you cried about it the moment you went home."

I did... A lot of times. So many times than I can count.

"You know, I respect your strength," he says as he squeezes my hand, "You survived all the tough times and made sure you built the future for you and your son. I'm sure he's grateful for you. Your son, that is."

I haven't heard anyone say those words to me. I needed them when I was pregnant. I needed them when my coworkers shunned me. I needed them when I felt too embarrassed to face my parents and sister.

To think that those kind words come from the one man responsible for my first heartbreak, I don't know how to feel about him.

"I know you think I'm the last person to say something like that, and I'm sure I'm the last person you want to hear from," he says, "but I really mean what I said, and it was not out of pity. I am just admiring you for being such a strong person and what you've accomplished."

"Thank you, Kevin," I say, smiling.

He smiles and realizes that he is still holding my hand, so he lets go. "I just wanted you to know," he smiles nervously. I can tell he is now getting uncomfortable for being so open and being nice to me.

"Do you want to see what he looks like?" I ask.

He turns to look at me, then nods, smiling.

I pull out my phone and look for the pictures I took before Alex left for the daycare this morning.

"Are you sure he isn't a girl?" Kevin teases as he turns his head to the side to make eye contact.

"Funny enough, I actually get that a lot," I chuckle softly. Alex's hair is getting long, and I need to give him a haircut soon.

"He's so adorable." He asks as he takes the phone and swipes to see more pictures. He stops swiping when he sees a photo of Alex and me in the hospital when Alex was born. I'm holding Alex in my arms with a bright smile.

I watch his smile get bigger as well.

"What's this?" I poke at his face, "Is everything okay? You can't stop smiling?"

"I'm not smiling," he says and returns the phone to me.

"Are you sure? I'm sure I saw you smiling," I tease him.

"You saw nothing," he insists.

"Fine then," I punch his shoulder, "Wimp."

He returns the punch to my shoulder but only weaker. He has a playful look on his face that matches my expression as well.

Age has started to show a little bit. When we first met, his hair was all dark, but now, a few strands of grey give him a sexier and mature look. His muscular physique shows that he has properly cared for his body for all these years.

He's quite the hunk, isn't he? He always has been.

He starts to lean in a little too close.

No, he's not the one moving closer... I am.

He notices it, and he moves in as well. The first touch was on my shoulder, then it turns into a grip on my body.

My vision starts to dim as I close my eyes.

My heart's pounding faster and faster.

The sound of his phone ringing breaks the trance. Bringing both of us back to our senses.

He clears his throat, "Excuse me." He gets up and takes the phone. He pauses and turns to look at me, "I think you're a wonderful mom."

"Thank you," I say to him.

He nods and answers the phone, "This better be important, James."

As he walks away from my view. I place my fingers on my lips. What was I about to do?

Chapter 6

In Her Eyes

Kevin

It's still fresh in my mind.

How soft her shoulder felt. Her naturally long eyelashes gently closed over her eyes. Her beautiful lips slowly parted as they anticipated the kiss that was about to happen.

My heart was pounding chaotically just from the anticipation of a kiss. It felt like I was running a thousand miles without being able to stop, and I never had a reaction like that before.

I could feel her breath on my face. She was panicking as well.

The phone call ruined the moment and broke me in half.

"Sir, we were able to get our talents the leading roles in the movie scheduled to be released the year after next," James announced.

"Oh, okay," was my honest reaction.

"Is everything all right, sir?" He asked, "You don't sound as excited as I thought you'd be. I mean, even with the scandal and your absence, we were still able to achieve this."

"Yeah, it's just I was in the middle of something important, and the timing of your call wasn't perfect," I explained.

"Oh, okay. You have something that's keeping you busy in Malibu?" He asked, "I thought you said you won't be able to leave the house."

"It's nothing, don't worry," I said to him, "If that's all, then no problem."

"Okay, enjoy the rest of your day, sir," James said before hanging up.

Lydia had left for the afternoon by the time I hung up the phone.

Even when she came back to prepare dinner, she didn't say anything about the attempted kiss, and I didn't even know how to bring it up.

I couldn't help but wonder if I had forgotten my skills as a playboy.

The next morning, I wake up and think about it again. The kiss. Well, the kiss that almost happened.

I make my way to the kitchen. Staring at the dining table isn't helping me to forget. She'll be here soon. I need to get out of this funk before she gets here.

The sound of the doorbell. She's early as usual. She lets herself in, dressed in a T-shirt and high-waist denim, showing off her curves.

"Good morning," she says warmly.

"Good morning," I reply, "You look really pretty this morning. What's the deal?"

She stares at herself and gives a complete 360°, "Huh? Nothing. I look normal wearing jeans and a T-shirt."

"Let's go with that," I shrug.

"What's your schedule like today?" She asks.

"I don't have any meetings," I reply, "So I'll just eat, watch TV, and sleep."

"For a billionaire, you actually sound very lazy," she says while shaking her head, "Have you left the house?"

"I can't risk the public seeing me," I reply, "I mean, you are aware of the scandal, aren't you?"

"Kevin, this Malibu. No one cares," she says in disbelief, "You need fresh air and sunlight."

"I'm good," I say with an exasperated sigh, making my way to the couch.

I lie down on the couch and turn on the TV, switching to the animal channel. A lion is about to begin her hunt.

Lydia stands in the way of my view.

"You are blocking my view," I say to her as I try to move around on the couch, but she keeps standing in front of me.

"You shouldn't be lying down on the couch this early in the morning," she says as she crosses her arms.

"I literally have nothing to do today," I remind her, "Oh, can I have some oatmeal with some fruits for breakfast? I don't even mind the instant kind with dried fruits."

She grabs me by the ear and pulls me out of the chair.

"Ouch! What the hell was that for?!" I yell.

"Go and make the oatmeal yourself," she orders.

"I don't take orders from you," I say to her as I get to my feet.

She's small, but her attitude surpasses my 6' 2" stature, maybe by an extra foot.

"It's my job to make sure my client is healthy," she explains.

"Yes, by making me food. Now shoo," I motion for her to move, "If you'll excuse me, I'm trying to watch a lion fight another lion for a chance to mate."

"Kevin..." she calls softly.

"What?"

ARROGANT BILLIONAIRE'S DO-OVER

She doesn't say anything, but her eyes start to plead with me.

"What exactly do you think you're doing?" I ask.

"I want you to exercise a little. You look like you are in really good shape, and I don't want you to lose your physique," she says.

I take a look at my body and back at her.

"Yes, I wouldn't want you to lose all this," she says as she presses her hands against my abs. Then she places her hand against my chest, rubbing gently.

"Do you really want to sit on the couch all day and lose this beautiful body of yours?" She asks.

I know it's just an attempt to make me do what she wants. I've been seduced by a lot of women, but I've never been fazed.

But the lilac smell from her hair dulls my senses. Her fingers against my abs and chest send me the sensations I cannot resist.

I wasn't safe at all.

"Fine, what do you want me to do?" I ask.

"I want you to come with me for a grocery shopping. You've been eating like a whale, and I need to go get a lot of food," she says.

"I'm pretty sure I don't eat that much. Thank you very much," I correct her with a frown.

"Right," she says sarcastically, "I just want you to accompany me on today's shopping trip."

"I think you might be forgetting something," I say with a dry chuckle, "I'm a billionaire and a celebrity. I don't go grocery shopping. The only shopping I might do is for a car or a house."

"Please, Kevin?" She pleads and even whimpers a little, "Just this once? If I buy a lot of things, I won't be able to carry them alone."

"I guess... I won't be a gentleman if I leave you to carry all the heavy lifting alone," I say with a shrug, "I'll go shower."

"You haven't even showered yet?" She asks in disbelief, "I thought super rich folks normally preach about getting up early to make the most of the day."

"Not this rich folk," I say with a smirk.

I'm ready to leave the house, and I notice she's already in her car, waiting for me. Come to think of it, I haven't actually paid attention to the car she comes to work with. It's a nice sedan. Not bad at all.

"What?" She asks as she straps herself in, noticing that I was yet to enter the car, "I swear to God if you're about to tell me a misogynistic joke about how a woman isn't a good driver."

"What? No," I shake my head, "I was going to say I expected a jeep."

"I don't have time to enjoy off-road adventures," she says, "I need only the bare minimum."

"Maybe so," I say as I get into the car.

She's a good driver. Well, she might be a little too cautious. She stays under the speed limit and checks both ways twice before making a turn. I must say I would be irritated if I were driving behind her while she always stays under the speed limit, and I have no idea why she looks both ways twice.

We arrive at the cafeteria, and just like she said earlier, no one cares about my presence.

Maybe it's because I'm wearing sunglasses and a baseball hat.

"Is the disguise necessary?" She asks.

"I can't have everyone in this store falling in love with me," I reply.

She snickers a little, "And why is that?"

"That's because I already have you in mind," I tease as I hold her chin and lift her head a little, bending down to get close to her face.

It's only a joke, but I notice the reddish tint on her ears.

I remember the attempt at a kiss yesterday and let go of her face.

"So what are we getting?" I ask, taking my eyes away from her and checking on everyone else in the store.

"Just fruits, vegetables, some meat, and extra ingredients," she replies in a shaky tone.

"What about spices?"

"I bought enough already," she replies.

The silence follows, and it's awkward.

"Let's get started," she says as she rubs her hands together.

Since I don't do my grocery shopping, I have no idea what she's doing. She talks about bargains, how to check for freshness, and whatnot, but all I can do is nod and smile. My smile is genuine, though.

Seeing her light up as she talks about which ingredient works with which to make the best meal warms my heart.

I didn't notice this years ago, but has she always been this bright?

I recall the photo of herself and her son in the hospital. The look of joy on her face really resonated with me, causing me to smile in return.

"Do you prefer turkey or chicken?" She asks as she shows me the packaged meat.

"What's the difference?"

"You don't know? Of course you wouldn't," she sighs, "Turkeys are bigger and, in my opinion, have more fat and taste better. But some say it makes them feel sleepy afterward, even though other meats also contain a similar amount of tryptophan, which causes sleepiness. Chicken generally feels dry unless..." she pauses and looks at me, "Are you listening to me at all?"

"You're very passionate about food," I reply, "I'm sorry for not noticing earlier. Maybe I noticed it but ignored it."

"You shouldn't be apologizing," she says softly, "The past is behind us."

"You're right. I'll have the turkey then."

"Wise choice, but do you have a special request for today's meals?"

"Turkey stew and pasta," I reply, "You'll join me for dinner, right?"

"Well, if you insist," she says, "I'll be there."

It's not like it's an official dinner date, but I'm excited about tonight's dinner.

We're getting ready to leave after the grocery shopping,

"We aren't going home just yet," she says.

"What? We already spent an hour here," I remind her, "We need to get going. I haven't had anything to eat."

"Calm down," she says as she touches my back, "We'll have brunch outside the house and then go home for dinner."

"Don't you need to pick up Alex from daycare?"

"His aunt has him," she replies, "Now stop creating excuses. Have you ever had a shawarma? It's similar to a gyro, but the toppings are different."

"No, I never had it," I reply.

"I know a good food truck," she says.

"I don't do street food," I politely try to decline.

"Don't judge until you try it," she says, "You'll love it, I promise."

"Fine."

It's strange. I've become too obedient to her lately. I need to make sure that I don't become completely docile...

The shawarma was heavenly, and I found myself having two.

The fun didn't stop there.

She took me to indoor rock climbing. We visited a small skating rink and watched others show off their skills.

I also had ice cream as well.

And now, it's past five pm, and she's driving us home, humming a tune I've never heard before. She didn't do anything like this when we were together years ago. So why now?

She turns to look at me and flashes a smile, "Did you have fun?"

"Is this part of the catering service?" I ask.

"You don't have to think too deeply about it," she says, "Like I said this morning, you just needed the sun and move around. And I really need help with the groceries."

"By the way, you didn't have to pay for the grocery items. Your assistant has included everything needed for your service, so the grocery is paid for," she explains.

"Oh, well, just tell the company to give you the money we spent today," I suggest.

"I'm good actually, this might even... never mind," she says.

She resumes her humming, and I just stare at her, completely mesmerized.

If I had taken our relationship more seriously eight years ago, would I have enjoyed more days like this?

It's too late to regret now.

Besides not being able to go grocery shopping, I also don't know how to cook properly. So she's insisted that I cook with her.

It's been fun.

As I cut the onion, I wipe my eyes furiously to stop the pain and the tears that keep coming out.

Her laughter isn't helping, either.

"Will you stop laughing?!" I yell in protest as I try to focus on chopping the onion.

"I'm sorry," she apologizes, but she can't stop giggling, "I should have given you the safety glasses. Also, did you know that if you cut the onion under running water, you won't have the problem you're having right now?"

"Why did you wait until now to tell me this information?" I ask as I glare at her.

She struggles to keep a straight face but breaks as she continues to laugh.

"Okay, that's it." I put down the knife and wash my hands.

"Wait, what are you doing?" She asks.

We are prepping the ingredients, so we haven't put anything on the fire, nor is the stove on.

"You'll find out soon," I say with an evil grin as I wipe my hands, "Remember, I know you're still ticklish."

"What?! No! Kevin, don't you dare," she warns, but she is still laughing, and I'm not taking her warning seriously.

She takes a few steps back while I take a few steps forward in her direction.

She runs away, and I start chasing her.

She's laughing and screaming, and I chase her around the dining table and into the living room. I tackle her onto the sofa and start tickling her sides.

"Kevin... stop, I can't... breathe!" She continued her hysterics, "I'm sorry... please."

I stopped the tickling, "Did you have enough laughter?"

"Yeah....yes, I have," she replies, trying to catch her breath.

"Good," I say.

While she's still trying to catch her breath, I'm still on her. Her shirt reveals her abs a little bit. It seems like I'm not the only one who kept in shape. She looks amazing.

She's still breathing hard, and the rise and fall of her breasts, which have gotten bigger, causes an aching within me.

Her breathing slows, and she looks at me. Her eyes tell me she is thinking about the same thing I'm thinking – yesterday's attempted kiss.

I want to kiss her.

Yesterday, she leaned in on her own accord. This time, I'm taking the lead.

I lean in close, my eyes open to see any signs of discomfort in her expression to make me stop.

But there are none.

Instead, her lips part slightly, and she raises her head a little to close the distance.

I brush my lips against hers, but for a second, I hesitate, thinking she wants me to stop. But she moves her head a little closer to take my retreating lips.

I pause and stare at her, and she nods.

We kiss.

Her arms circle around my neck to keep me from retreating.

I kiss her back a little deeper. She holds my lower lip captive, sucking on me intensively.

I place my hand on her belly, and she shudders. She always had a sensitive belly.

Her gentile moans seep into my mouth, sending direct signals to my brain.

It's taking everything in me not to undress her completely and take her right now. I don't want to rush this.

She stops the kiss and whispers, "Neck..."

I kiss her neck, and she lets out a sigh of relief. Her fingers behind my head stroke my hair gently.

I continue to feast on her neck.

She opens her legs, locking me between them.

I let go of her neck and return to her lips. Her hands find their way into my shirt, and she starts to claw on my back.

That's new.

It's bliss.

The kiss continues until we're both out of breath.

As we finally let go of each other's lips, I stare into her eyes.

Just when our desires get more intense, my stomach starts to grumble, interrupting the mood that we finally got going.

I laugh at the situation, and she joins in, too.

"Well, we finally got that out of our system," I say with relief as I get off her body and help her up.

"Your meal will be in a smaller potion. You were too heavy back there," she says with a groan as she tries stretching her body.

"Let's get dinner going," she says.

"No problems," I reply.

I'm now grateful for the scandal Sandra caused.

Chapter 7

Precious Little One

Kevin

I can still feel her tongue in my mouth. I'm hesitant to brush my teeth because I don't want to forget the sensation.

She stayed for dinner, but there was no goodbye kiss. I probably won't remember how the kiss felt by tomorrow morning.

Or so I thought.

I wake up the next morning and suddenly remember the sensation of her lips.

Now, I don't know if I'm to ignore my oral hygiene just for the sake of remembering a kiss. Come on, Kevin. Get hold of yourself. It's just a kiss. I've had many – too many to count.

ARROGANT BILLIONAIRE'S DO-OVER

So why is her kiss so special?

Is it because it made my heart pound? Or is it because there is a chance that I will never experience the kiss again?

Whatever the reason is, it's making me delusional. I need to get on with my life.

After brushing my teeth, I do a quick workout routine.

And no, it's not because she mentioned I was getting heavier or she liked how my body looked.

I just want to stay fit so when I return to New York, women will fall in love with me again.

Hum..., going back to New York? Do I want to go back?

"I'm going to check if there are any gyms around here," I say to myself, ignoring any negative self-talk in my head.

I check the time on my phone, and it's past nine am.

She's late.

My phone starts ringing and it's her number.

"You're late," I say to her immediately as I answer the phone.

"I'm really sorry, there's an emergency event, and Peak Bites needs all hands on deck," she explains, "But there's a problem."

"Okay?"

"I can't find someone to watch over Alex. The daycare had to close temporarily due to too many sick kids, and my sister isn't in the state today," she continues, "So I'm just trying to find a babysitter. I'll make you breakfast before I go to Peak Bites."

"Why don't you bring Alex here?" I ask.

"What?"

"Alex. Bring him over. I'll watch over him," I explain.

She goes silent, and I can tell that she's wondering if I'm responsible enough to take care of her son.

"It'll be fine. He's an angel, isn't he?" I ask, "Any allergy I should worry about?"

"He doesn't have any allergies," she replies, "He's a little stubborn though. But very sweet."

Gee, I wonder where he got the stubbornness from?

"You just thought of something rude, didn't you?" She asks.

"No, I'm just thinking about how fun it'll be having him here," I quickly defend.

"I don't know...," she whispers.

"It'll be fine." I insist.

ARROGANT BILLIONAIRE'S DO-OVER

"All right, so he shouldn't have too much sugar," she says while kissing Alex's forehead multiple times.

The poor boy is completely smothered by his mom. Lucky fellow.

"Make sure he takes his nap by 1 pm after lunch. He eats lunch around noon. Don't let him sleep too long. He typically wakes up on his own in an hour," she continues the instructions as she squeezes him in a hug for the third time, "Also, I brought some juice boxes..."

"You didn't, mommy," Alex says, "We left it at home."

"What?" She asks and checks the backpack she brought along, and she sinks into despair, "I'll go home and get it."

"Lydia, I'll get the juice. You don't have to worry," I assure her.

"Thank you. Send me the bill for everything you buy, and I'll refund you," she says.

Did she just forget I'm a billionaire?

"Okay, Alex, mommy loves you," she says to her boy and kisses him again, "Don't give Uncle Kevin any problems."

"Okay, mommy," he says with a smile.

She finally lets him go, and we both watch her drive away.

As she disappears from our view, I turn to him, "So, what should we do first?"

"I want to pee."

Go figure...

Alex is into coloring books and reading. I'm just watching him complete another colorful masterpiece. He doesn't speak much and doesn't even run around.

Just sits, colors, and reads. I left the channel on a show for kids his age, but he'd only occasionally glance at the TV and then back to his books.

"Juice," he demands. Well, he certainly inherited his mother's bossy nature...

"Let's go buy some juice," I reply as I get up to leave.

We get to the door, and he doesn't follow me to the car.

"We need to go," I say to him.

"Up," he says as he raises both arms towards me.

"Aren't you four?"

"Up."

"The car is right there...."

"UUUUP!"

"Okay, fine, jeez," I let out a groan and pick him up, heading to my car.

He was surprisingly light despite his chubby cheeks. I expected a little more weight. He felt cuddly at the same time. Now I understand why his mother is so fond of holding him.

"You're grumpy," he remarks as he pokes my face, maybe hoping to get a reaction from me.

"And you should stop poking me," I reply.

He pauses, only to smirk and continue his poking as if my words have no power over him.

We got to the mall, and his excitement increased.

"Rocket," he pointed at the kiddie ride.

"We have to go home soon for your lunch and nap," I remind him, checking the time; it's a few minutes to noon.

"Please, just a little," he pleads.

I check the watch again, "I don't think she won't mind if we were a few minutes late. Why not?"

I put some money in for the ride, and it seems like he's having the time of his life on the rocket ride. His laughter makes me smile.

I look around and realize a lot of people are present with their kids. Did they all go to the same daycare?

"Daddy, can I go next?" A kid standing next to us asks his father.

"All right, let's wait for his turn to end, and then you'll get on," his father replies.

As Alex gets down from the ride, we leave to get the juice as he had earlier requested. He holds a juice box while sitting on my shoulders as we continue exploring the mall.

We play a wack-a-mole game several times and then watch a movie.

I give him some ice cream and pray that he won't get a sugar rush. Throughout the mall, we notice many families with small kids.

"Uncle Kevin?" He calls.

"Yes?"

"Do you have a dad?" He asks.

My old man.

"I used to have a dad," I reply, "But he's no longer with us."

"I don't have a dad, either," he replies, "But all my friends do."

"Do you feel bad about it?" I ask.

"No, not really. I'm happy with Mommy and Aunt Lily," he replies with a giggle, "Aunty Lily is like you. Grumpy. But I like her."

"Do you like me?" I ask.

"Ice cream," he replies without hesitation.

"If your plan is to bribe me to get what you want, then you have no idea what it's like to work in the competitive entertainment industry," I say with a smirk, "Also, that shouldn't be the way you make people do what you want okay?"

ARROGANT BILLIONAIRE'S DO-OVER

"Okay."

"I'm sure your mom gives you whatever you want when you beg enough times, am I right?" I ask.

"Yes!" He replies and starts kicking his feet, "Ah, but if I do anything bad, she yells at me."

I'm a little worried that the little rascal gets away with everything he wants. But then again, someone as strict as Lydia won't let that sort of behavior fly all the time.

"Try not to make things too hard for your mom, okay?" I request.

"Okay," he agrees, "Uncle Kevin, do you like mommy?"

I stop walking and strain my neck upwards to look at him, "Why do you ask?"

"Because if you like mommy, then I see you more, then you get me treats," he explains with childlike innocence.

"You're just using me for personal gain, aren't you?" I let out an exhausted sigh and continue walking, "I like your mommy. But don't tell her, okay? Promise?"

"Promise," he agrees.

Do I like Lydia? As an adult, one may mistake an emotion like infatuation for love. The majority of my love life has been dominated by infatuation.

I find a woman attractive, and then I get involved. After wine and dine and some hot sex, I move on to the next. One may think such a lifestyle is a flex, but is it, really?

I saw a lot of happy fathers today. Sure, we may not be of equal class, financially speaking, but compared to them, am I really living a happy life?

Do they have to run to a different location because of some scandal blasted in the media? Do they want to wake up feeling empty after spending the night partying and having fun? Do they return home and find there's no one to greet them after a long day of hard work?

The answer to all my questions was probably no.

I once told Lydia that being a playboy was beneficial for keeping my appearance as the head of a talent agency.

But Lydia became the best chef at Peak Bites solely with her talent and hard work and didn't have to seduce anyone to achieve her dreams.

Maybe I've been doing it all wrong. No, I know for sure I've been doing it wrong.

"Sleepy..." Alex's slurred speech interrupts my thoughts, so I bring him down from my shoulders and place his head against my chest.

We bought a lot of things, and I've torn up the receipts, so Lydia won't find out how much I spent exactly.

The drive home is shorter yet peaceful. The gentle snore of the little one calms my senses, and I don't mind hearing it longer.

After we arrive home, I put Alex on the guest bed, and I lay on the edge of the bed to avoid him falling. I wonder if he is comfortable as almost every bed in this house is hard as a rock.

As I lay next to him, I can't help but admire the effort Lydia had put into raising this child on her own.

After a long day together, I fell asleep.

Chapter 8

Budding Desires

Lydia

Night Of The Kiss

As I recall what I did this evening at his house, my face turns a shade of rose red from blushing. I promised myself I would never fall for a man again, but now I can't resist my desire. I want him so badly.

I know I'm only fooling myself.

He is acting like he cares about me because he is taking a break from his usual lifestyle to avoid the attention of the media due to the scandal.

I'm just a convenient emotional dump nearest to him, as he can't contact any of his previous lovers.

He seems like he's changed a bit, though. He did go grocery shopping with me today. In the past, he would have left it to me to do that alone, giving me his card. Not only did he come along for grocery shopping, but he also tried shawarma from the food truck, went indoor rock climbing, went skating, and enjoyed ice cream.

I still remember his laughter, and his smile still burns a bright image in my mind.

No, no, no... I can't be fooled. I mustn't be fooled.

But the harder I try to convince myself that he hasn't changed, the more I think I'm lying to myself. Why is it that? Because a part of me knows that I see other things that are different about him today.

He never showed interest in cooking in the past, but suddenly, he wanted me to teach him how to cook.

He was playful and even ticked me, making us both laugh. We had numerous passionate moments eight years ago without having sex, but it was during that moment I realized how easy it would have been for him to get me to spread my legs.

I would have been upset years ago, but I wasn't even bothered this evening.

My head searches for logical answers, but my heart screams for Kevin. My ears didn't know what to listen to, and my mind refused to pick a side.

I want him. But he's still a playboy.

He's gotten nicer. But I don't want to get hurt again.

He might have matured to take the relationship more seriously. I'm not even sure.

"Mom?" Alex's sweet voice pierces my thoughts.

I lift my eyes and stare at the beautiful angel, rubbing his eyes as he wakes up.

"You're back?" He asks with a yawn.

"Yes, I am," I reply as I open my arms wide enough for him to embrace me. He smiles softly and rushes in for the hug, "Why are you waking up? Kiddo?" I ask, "Or are you just missing mommy?"

"I'm thirsty," he answers.

"Oh," my shoulders drop at his response, "You don't miss mommy?"

"I do," he assures me.

Alex. He is my reminder to not trust any man who has no desire to commit to the relationship. I help my little prince get his drink, then tuck him back into bed.

The sound of my phone ringing draws my attention. My boss is calling. It's a little late, and he only calls if it's an emergency.

"Hello, sir?" I answer, "Good evening."

"Good evening," he responds, "Can you make breakfast for the client you've been assigned to earlier in the morning and come to Peak Bites?"

His voice sounds stressed and in a state of panic.

"Sure, I can. What's the matter?"

"Well, the mayor is having a big party, and we've been tasked with catering service at the last minute," he explains, "I can't let this slip. He specifically asked for you, but I have to warn you, we'll be short-staffed to handle this order." He pauses to breathe and relax, "That's basically the gist. I'll see you tomorrow."

He hangs up the phone before I can refuse. Well, it's not like I will refuse my boss's request, but I just want to spend more time with Kevin.

Oh, God... What am I saying?

"I must be losing my mind...," I say with an exasperated sigh, then I place a finger on my neck where he'd kissed. I'm getting all frustrated because of a stupid kiss.

It's morning, and Alex is awake.

I can hear the sound of the TV in the living room.

As I try to check my phone, I notice several missed calls from Mariam. There are also a few from Lily.

Strange. Fearing something might be wrong, I call the daycare center.

"He-hello?" I greet half-asleep as I stretch, stifling a yawn and enduring the shaky feeling of my legs. Maybe I should have waited a couple more minutes until I was more awake before calling.

"Ms. Johnson?" Mariam replies, "I've been trying to reach you."

"I noticed," I remark, "What's the problem? Is everything all right?"

"I forgot to tell Lily to inform you, but the daycare won't be open today and tomorrow," she explains.

My sleepiness disappears instantly as I sit upright.

"Why, what happened?" I asked.

"Too many kids are sick, and a couple of our staff called in sick," she explains, "Based on our health regulation policy, we won't be able to open the daycare today and tomorrow. We'll resume on Monday, assuming the situation is better."

"Oh, no," my shoulders drop, and I groan in frustration.

"I'm so sorry. Another busy day?" She asks.

"Frightfully so. I need to be at Peak Bites today," I explain, "I'll just ask Lily to watch over Alex."

"Oh uh... I'm not sure that's possible," she says, "Your sister is going to be in Chicago today. She is attending a seminar there."

"Oh, did you know about Lily's plan?"

ARROGANT BILLIONAIRE'S DO-OVER

"No, I didn't. She just told me about it this morning when I called her after I left you a message. I was hoping your sister could be available to watch Alex." She replies nervously.

Uh-huh, that's why Lily was calling me, also.

"Mommy, I'm hungry," Alex says, running into the room.

"Just give me a minute, sweetie. Have you brushed your teeth," I ask, and he shakes his head, "Okay, just hold on."

He climbs onto the bed and embraces me while waiting for me to finish my call.

"I know a few good babysitters. I can recommend them," Mariam suggests.

"I'm not too comfortable with a stranger in my home, caring for my baby alone," I admit. I'm sure they are good babysitters, but leaving Alex alone with someone I don't know makes me worry.

"Do you know anyone else?" Mariam asks.

"I'll ask around. If it doesn't work, I'll call you to get the contact information for the babysitters you can recommend," I answer.

"All right, once again, I apologize for any inconvenience this may have caused," she apologizes, "I'll be waiting for your response."

"Thank you."

I end the call and figure out who to ask for help.

Mom's in Chicago.

Friends, friends... Yikes, I don't have a lot of friends I can call to get help.

That's it, Allison!

I quickly dialed Allison. She's off this week, so I'm assuming the boss didn't call her for help with this event.

"Hey there," she answers. Her tone is cold but not mean.

She's been crying again. Her husband is the sweetest man I know, so I can only guess why she's crying.

I'm feeling uncomfortable asking now. I don't want to remind her of her pain.

"Is everything all right?" I ask.

She's quiet at first, and then the sobbing resumes, "It failed.... Another IVF failed."

"I'm sorry," I apologize. There's nothing else I can do but apologize.

"Why are you apologizing?" With a dry chuckle, she asks, "I'm going to be fine. What do you need?"

"Oh, I..."

Quick. Think of something else to say.

"The boss asked me to come to Peak Bites. It seems we're short-handed for the mayor's event," I explain, "I wanted to know if you were coming too."

"He didn't contact me, probably because it's my week off," she says, "I feel bad for you; you'll be stuck with those snotty little brats without me to protect you."

"I'll be fine. I'll be really busy, so ignoring them will be easy peasy," I assure her, "Just take good care of yourself and Chris."

"Yeah, I'll try," she says, "Take care and good luck."

I whisper 'goodbye' and end the call.

"Mummy, hungry," Alex reminds me, "Late for daycare."

"No, sweetie, there's no daycare today," I explain.

After getting Alex breakfast, I was running out of time and left him in the hands of Kevin.

I'm worried.

While I'm maintaining my calm on the surface, watching over the other chefs, and keeping everything under control, I'm worried.

Years ago, Kevin made it clear that he had no intention to have kids. With his grumpy attitude, I'm worried he might lose his patience with Alex.

I sigh.

"Is everything all right, Chef Johnson," the mayor asks.

He's here to check on our progress. I have no idea why, but some clients insist on appearing while we work. They want to see what we're doing with their money, which is all good and acceptable, but it's different when they're powerful men or women. They make us nervous.

Looking around, I notice some of the cooks are apprehensive about his presence. And my haters? Well, I've gotten used to their glares and whispers.

"Yes, everything is fine, Mayor," I reply with a friendly smile.

"Good, good," he nods in satisfaction before turning his eyes to the meat pies I'm stuffing, "I told your boss that I need you here if the meals are to be a success. I'm glad he honored my request."

"Thank you for requesting me," I bow and focus on my meal.

While I appreciate his praise, it doesn't help my career at Peak Bites. When I started working at Peak Bites, the owner welcomed me with open arms. But after some of his clients started to request me, he became a little cold.

I became more popular, and his best clients, like the mayor, started booking me for their events. I can smell the jealousy, but with the number of customers and the revenue I bring in, he can't afford to let go of me.

I read somewhere that one should never outshine the boss, but I don't know what to do. I still want my clients to be happy with what I make.

I can't afford not to do my best at my work. I have a son to take care of.

"My offer for you to work as my private chef is still available, though," he reminds me.

I can feel the stares. Although it's his second time making this request, this is the first time he's saying it in front of my colleagues. And most of them aren't too excited to hear about it.

"I respectfully decline once more," I say to him, "Peak Bites is where I am meant to be." I resist the urge to add, 'For now.'

"While I appreciate your visit, I fear I may not be able to focus properly on cooking, and I don't want the meals to turn out poorly," I say to him, "And I know just how much you love our meat pies."

He stares at the meat pies and back at me; a smirk forms on his face, "My offer still stands either way. Excuse me."

He turns, leaving me with the judging eyes of my colleagues. Even my boss doesn't look that pleased.

I wish Allison were here.

I need to finish up and return to my angel. His smile will be enough to lift this mood.

Maybe I should quit and join the mayor as his personal chef. But that would definitely raise some brows. I can always start a gourmet food truck or my own catering service. I don't need to deal with the boss or my colleagues looking at me with envy.

9 pm.

The event ended later than I expected. The mayor and his wife ask me if I can stay longer to socialize with their guests, but they let me go after hearing my excuse that I need to pick up my son from a babysitter,

I'm at Kevin's house. I ring the doorbell, and there's no response. I remember Kevin said I could come in without knocking, so I come in and follow the sound of the TV.

I walk into the living room, and it's a mess. There are a lot of toys that weren't there before. I see empty juice boxes, an ice cream container, and a pizza box with half-eaten slices on the coffee table. There are pieces of paper beside the table with different crayon drawings on them.

I find Alex and Kevin lying on the floor, with their legs kicking the air behind them, their hands on pencils, drawing on some more paper. The sight instantly warms my heart.

Kevin stops drawing and looks over at Alex. He's smiling at my son. I haven't seen him smile like that before. A soft, sincere smile filled with love and admiration. A smile that says he adores Alex.

Stop, Lydia. You're just exhausted. Don't be stupid.

I can barely hear anything except the song playing on the TV and the sound of my heartbeat. I lean against the wall and continue watching them. I can't stop smiling.

A devious smirk appears on Alex's face as he rushes to color Kevin's paper.

"Hey!" Kevin pouts and then tackles the five-year-old but slowly so he doesn't injure him before placing his mouth on the boy's stomach and blowing raspberries.

Alex's giggles fill the air, and I cover my mouth to suppress my chuckle.

My son notices me, "Mommy!"

Kevin also turns and notices me. He tries to compose himself, putting on a more serious face, but it's too late to look cool now because I've already seen how much fun they've been having.

As Kevin lets go of him, Alex runs to me with an action figure, "Mommy, Uncle Kelvin got me this."

"It's Uncle Kevin," I say, correcting Alex.

"Uncle Kevin," Alex says as he shows me the toy.

"Did you say thank you?" I ask.

"Mm-hmm," he nods in response.

I look over at Kevin, and he only shrugs, still keeping that serious expression on his face.

"All right, sweetie, go get your backpack. Mama had a long day," I say to Alex.

He stares at the toy and back to me with a sad look.

"We're going home with everything Uncle Kevin got you," I assure him, and a smile comes back to his face.

"Thank you!" He hugs me and rushes to find his backpack.

I turn my attention to the babysitter, "How much did everything cost?"

"Don't bother, consider them all his birthday gifts I missed out on," he replies.

He sounds like he is Alex's estranged father, trying to make peace.

"Thank you for tonight," I say with a bow.

He gives me a quizzical look and holds my chin, forcing me to look at him, "You really had a rough day today, didn't you?"

I take a deep breath and exhale, "I want to take a nice bath while some grapes are fed to me by a male Greek supermodel."

"Will a white billionaire playboy work?" He teases.

"Nice try Casanova," I smirk.

Normally, I move my head away, but we keep eye contact. He's leaning closer hesitantly. He wants to kiss me again, but he's unsure. He's more considerate about how I feel than he used to. In the past, he'd just grabbed me and kissed me whenever he wanted.

We're both trying to figure out if we're ready to face each other's feelings again.

I do want to kiss him. The recent kiss has begun to fade as the possibility of the next kiss draws near.

"Mom! I'm ready," Alex announces, causing us to separate.

"All right, let's get going," I say to him.

"I'll drive you home," Kevin offers.

"I have a car," I remind him. "Are you suggesting you drive us home using my car and then take a cab back?"

"Sounds like a plan," he shrugs, but I can see the excitement in his eyes.

Honestly, why weren't you this cute and vulnerable eight years ago?

"Thank you, kind gentleman," I say to him, "But you've already done enough for today. I'm really grateful."

"Don't mention it," he says.

I know he has more to say as he walks us to my car.

"What is it?" After strapping Alex in, I ask, "I know you have something you want to say. You can go ahead and tell me."

"Can you bring Alex along? Whenever he doesn't have daycare?" He asks.

"Oh?" I raise a brow and let the smirk grow, "Is someone attached to my baby now? I thought you don't like kids?"

"I never said I didn't like kids," he defends, "But Alex, he's a better company than you are."

I roll my eyes, "Yeah, right."

I get in the car and start the engines.

He waves us goodbye, and I drive off. I can still see him watching us through the rearview mirror until he disappears.

"I like Uncle Kevin," Alex says.

"Is that so? Well, Uncle Kevin seems to like you too," I tease.

"He also says he likes you," Alex says, then stops talking when he realizes something, "Oh no, Uncle Kevin said not to tell you."

"It's fine," I assure him.

"Do you like Uncle Kevin?" He asks.

"Mommy's not sure," I admit.

Mommy's not sure, really.

Chapter 9

Father's Day

Kevin

It's June: Father's Day is coming up., and lately, I've really been feeling like one. It's presumptuous of me, but Alex has been visiting me more often, and I feel like we've connected.

Lydia's shift continues as usual: she arrives early for breakfast, except this time, she leaves in the afternoon to bring Alex over. I tease her for it, saying she was hesitant to leave Alex with me at first, but now she doesn't have any problem bringing Alex here.

Lydia replies, saying she only decided to do so because her sister is still in Chicago, and there is no one else to watch over Alex. It may be an attempt to hurt my ego, but I know Alex loves spending time with me, and she is happy that she can bring him here.

I've started to fall for her harder than I expected. I'm trying to convince myself that I'm experiencing this feeling for Lydia because no other women are around me, but I know that's the lie I keep repeating to myself. I shake off my thoughts and try to read through the reports from my office.

"Fuck!" I hear her yell, accompanied by the sound of metal clanging to the floor.

I rush to find her upset in the kitchen. It seems she accidentally spilled the chili she was preparing on her and her outfit.

"I'll clean the kitchen. You can use my bathroom to clean up yourself," I say, and Lydia doesn't give her witty comebacks this time.

While she showers and changes her clothes with chili splash, I finish cleaning the mess in the kitchen. On a side note, I've also become addicted to cleaning. I plan to continue this newly acquired habit when I return to New York.

"I borrowed your dress shirt," Lydia says.

My mouth almost drops as she steps into the living room. Her hair is still wet, and she is drying her hair with the towel hanging on her shoulders.

She turns her attention to me, continuing to squeeze the hair dry. I stare at her from head to toe. I take note of the clothing clinging to her breasts. Her hips prove that the upper part of her breast isn't the only part that has grown after all these years.

"Stop staring," she says as she tosses the towel at me while pouting.

I make no attempts to dodge the towel and let it cover my face, helping to temporarily break the spell that her body has cast over me. As I pull down the towel, she's working her hair into a ponytail. The shirt slowly ascends, revealing some of her beautiful thighs.

When she's done with the hair, she turns to me and says, "I'll have to start from scratch; just give me a few more minutes."

"Why don't you take a break and sit next to me," I ask.

She gives me a suspicious look, "What are you up to?"

"As a customer, I only want what's best for my chef," I defend, "I think you deserve a little break. I'm not hungry yet, and you have to pick up Alex in an hour. So just take a little break."

"Huh," she smirks, "Is that so?" She makes her way to the chair and sits beside me, crossing her legs and exposing more skin. Her fingers seductively dance across the exposed flesh.

"Since your intentions for me to take a break are pure, I'm sure this has no effect whatsoever on you," she says in a sultry voice.

She's got me. I swallow hard, but I don't look away, nor do I respond.

"Nothing?" She asks, raising her brow to show she's impressed. Then she lets out a sigh, signifying that she's given up on tempting me.

While I'm grateful she put a break to help me restrain myself, a part of me wants her to continue teasing me until I can't contain myself.

While she focuses her attention on the TV, I admire her beauty, taking my breath away. I look at her lips, and I remember how they felt on my lips. There hasn't been any attempt to kiss after the night with Alex. Even though I've seen her looking at me or staring at my lips like I am currently doing, I haven't been convinced enough that she wants me again.

"You've changed," she says.

"Have I? I think I've always been this way," I say with arrogance.

She looks at me amused, "You don't even sound as arrogant as you used to."

What? I don't...?

"I still find it hard to believe," she starts to explain, "You help me cook, you clean, Alex loves you, I haven't seen you make calls to other women like you used to when we were together." She pauses and chuckles, "I guess we were never truly together back then, so I guess you were right. You were free to do what you wanted."

"I did that?" I ask.

She doesn't answer, but the look on her face confirms my question. What she said was something I've done many times. Back then, I was showing off how easy it was for me to get a new girl. And now, I realize how shameful and demeaning my actions were to her.

And here I am, thinking of trying to get a life with her. I'm the absolute worst.

"Well, I'm glad that you've changed," she says and gets up. As she stretches, I get a faint glimpse of the teal underwear, "In the end, it might only be a temporary situation. You can't leave the house because of the scandal and can't contact any of your lovers. You might be acting docile until you're ready to return to your normal life in New York, where you are king."

As usual, her words leave a dent in my heart. She has her reasons for saying that. Anyone in her shoes would think the same. She is willing to tell it where it hurts.

"Lydia..." I call softly.

"Yes?" She replies, awaiting my defense.

I can't say anything. My words won't mean much to her. I can make the promises, but will Lydia be willing to hear them? How will my words be enough to convince her that I changed?

"I was only teasing you," she says as she sticks out her tongue at me, "Jeez, you've become stiffer than before." Even though she is smiling, I know it wasn't totally a joke.

My assistant and the PR team are almost done with resolving the scandal issue, so my chances of returning to New York soon are very likely. Once I go back, it's easy to return to the lifestyle I used to have. But I don't want to. That lifestyle has no true peace.

I might be feeding my delusions, but I kind of like the life I'm currently leading right now. I have someone I care about who cooks my meals and keeps me company. I have a child that I can picture as mine. When Lydia pitched the idea of getting married and having a family eight years ago, I thought it would be a waste of time. But now, I've started to appreciate it.

It's past two in the afternoon. I'm watching entertainment news, and my scandal is dying down. Sandra made an apology video, so I'm contemplating if I should respond.

"This case should last a little longer," I can't help admitting. *Hmmm, I really have become used to life here.*

The sound of a car pulling into the driveway informs me Lydia and Alex are here. She left to pick him up from the daycare an hour ago. As the front door opens, I can hear Lydia saying reassuring words to him. They enter the living room, and I notice the weary expressions on mother and son's faces.

"Hey Alex," I greet the young man.

"Hi, Uncle Kelvin," he replies. Usually, I'd correct him, but there are better times for that. He has his eyes on the ground, looking sad.

"All right, sweetie, go wash your face upstairs and change your clothes," Lydia instructs softly.

He nods and heads upstairs to one of the rooms that Lydia uses for her breaks. She watches him leave, and her shoulders sink.

"What happened?" I ask.

ARROGANT BILLIONAIRE'S DO-OVER

She takes a deep breath and turns to me, "It's just something at his daycare."

"Okay?"

"You know Father's Day is coming up, right?"

"Oh, is it? Wasn't it in last month?" I ask.

"What? No. Mother's Day is in May," she sighs and steers me back to the topic, "This month is when we have Father's Day."

"Oh," I say; I pause, realizing what seems to be the problem, "*Oh...*"

"Yeah," she says, "The daycare is asking the fathers to come tomorrow and last year, Alex was the only one without a father figure, and he feels bad about it."

Of course, he will.

"Do you have a dad?" He had asked me before. When I answered him that I no longer have a dad, he told me it didn't bother him that he doesn't have a father. But I'm sure it bothered him when he looked at the other kids, realizing he was the only one without a father figure at the daycare.

Seeing him sad is causing my heart to hurt.

You really have changed, haven't you, Kevin? Lydia was right.

I have an idea. "Can I go with him?" I ask.

She turns to look at me, and the moody expression on her face quickly disappears, "What?"

"Can I go with him to the daycare tomorrow?" I ask again.

"I thought you came to Malibu to lay low?" She asks.

"The scandal is already dying down, and if I give them…" I rub my index finger and thumb together to show what I mean, "I'm sure they won't say anything about me being at the daycare."

"You're going to bribe people to avoid any media attention?" She asks, still confused.

"I may not have to do anything," I explain, "I might be a celebrity, but I just own a talent agency. People tend to recognize actors and actresses, but they don't know us. Also, as I've mentioned, the scandal is already dying down, and people might have forgotten about it already."

"I can't risk my son's quiet life at the daycare," she insists, crossing her arms.

"Trust me," I say, trying to convince her. She doesn't want to but at the same time…

"Mom, I'm done changing," Alex says, drawing our attention to him. He doesn't seem any better. The sparkle he usually has after changing isn't there either. He walks past his mom and sits next to me on the sofa.

"I must be losing my mind," I can hear her grumble. After a big sigh, she asks, "Alex, do you want Uncle Kevin to come with you tomorrow?"

"Can he?" Alex smiles. The joy starts to return to his eyes, but he turns to look at me, a bit confused, "But you aren't my dad."

ARROGANT BILLIONAIRE'S DO-OVER

Ouch! Why does that hurt my feelings?

"Well, I can also go as an uncle," I explain, "They just want you to be with a father figure, and that means any person who is like a father can go.

"Oh," he says in realization, "Then I want you to come. Is that okay, mommy?"

"Well, it was my idea," she answers with a shrug.

"Thank you," he says, beaming with smiles. There's the sound of his tummy growling, causing him to chuckle gleefully, "I'm hungry."

"I'll make something for all of us," Lydia says as she makes her way to the kitchen. As she leaves, she motions for me to follow her.

"I'll be right back," I say to Alex, then follow after her.

"You called?" I ask, making my way to her as she pulls out the ingredients for lunch.

"I don't know what you're planning to do, but Alex is my world," she says. I suppose I need to convince her I'm not using Alex just to get to her. I adore Alex, and I have no intention of hurting him in any way.

"Lydia, it's not like that even in the slightest ways," I assure her, "I'm only doing this because I want to make him feel better. I'm growing quite fond of him, and I don't want to see him upset. That's all."

"Are you sure?" She narrows her eyes.

I smirk and place my index finger directly under her chin. "You know how I do things. If I want to score points, I go directly to the goal. I don't need any shortcuts."

"As usual, you're full of yourself," she says in defiance as she moves her head away, but I grab her neck and pull her gently close to my face.

She's startled but continues looking at me like I am no threat. I like it. I love it. While my hand rests on her nape, I use my left thumb to gently stroke behind her ear, putting her in an almost hypnotic state. The glare in her eyes is a sign of a level of no resistance.

'Bring it on.' That is what her eyes are trying to tell me.

"You aren't so tough, you know?" I remark.

"And you aren't so charming either," she shoots back.

I lean in and kiss her neck. Her gasp of surprise thrills me to hear.

"Dirty player," she smirked as she grabbed my hair and tried to pull me away. I switch to using my teeth gently, sinking into her. She stops pulling, and instead, she starts caressing my hair gently.

I pin her against the counter and lift my left leg, rubbing against her inner thighs. It's an attempt to test if she'll accept my move. As she lowers her hips, grinding slowly against my thighs, I can tell my move has been accepted.

"And that's just it," I say to her as I pull away from her.

She quickly grabs me by my collar, "Why... Don't stop..."

"Mommy, what's for lunch?" Alex asks from the living room, almost on cue.

"Shoot," she murmurs as she lets me go, "I'll be making some lasagna." She gives me an annoyed look, and I notice her cheeks are bright red, "Jerk."

I hold her nape, and this time, I only bite the tip of her ear, making her flinch. Then I whisper, "As I was saying, I won't use Alex to get to you. I may be a playboy, but I'm no coward."

"A playboy *is* a coward," she says softly as she struggles to free herself from my grip.

"But here I am, facing you, and you're responding," I remind her what has just happened.

She says nothing to defend herself, so I let her go. A wicked smile remains on my face.

"I'll watch over Alex tomorrow," I promise her, "He'll be fine, I promise."

"He better be," she warns, "Or you'll have to deal with a situation far worse than the scandal you're dealing with."

"And what case would that be? May I ask?"

It's her turn to smile wickedly, "Dealing with an angry mom."

Maybe it's her attempt to frighten me. It would have worked if we hadn't been on the verge of making out a few minutes ago.

Today is the day. Alex is excited, and I share in his excitement. I've never been to the daycare, so Lydia is driving us there.

"And then, it's story time, and then we'll play with toys, and then..." Alex continues to tell me everything that will happen today. I pay attention to him with the same excitement. I still haven't gotten tired of listening to him.

Each activity he mentioned makes me a little more excited. It reminds me of the time my father planned to take me to the zoo. On the way to the zoo, I told my dad about all the animals I wanted to see. I vividly remember he listened to me without interrupting with a big smile on his face.

When I got older, I didn't understand why he was happy just listening to me. But now, as I listen to Alex, I'm starting to realize what my father was seeing.

"If you tell him everything, then you might ruin his experience," Lydia advises.

Instead of sitting in the passenger seat, I chose to stay behind with Alex so I could listen to him rant.

"Let him tell me everything. I'm not a big fan of surprises," I tell her, "It's my first time doing something like this. I would like to do anything to embarrass him."

She wants to say something but shakes her head. I can see the smirk from the rearview mirror, and I can only guess what she is saying.

"Hopefully, the scandal doesn't embarrass him." While she may have said it as a joke, there's a chance it might happen. *Crap, now I'm actually feeling nervous.*

We arrive at the daycare, and it's smaller than I expected. I can already recognize some of the men. They were with their children at the mall on the day the daycare was closed.

"There you are," a lady announces as she walks over to us; she stops to look at me, a polite smile on her face, and nods to acknowledge my presence before returning her attention to Lydia, "Who is this handsome man?"

"Hi, Mariam," Lydia returns the greeting, "This not-so-handsome man will be here to accompany my Alex for the Father's Day event."

"Oh," Mariam says at first, then the realization sets in as she stares at the three of us standing together, "Oh, I get it." She says while winking at Lydia.

"I have a feeling you're misunderstanding the situation, but meh, whatever," Lydia gives up without a fight. It's nice to know I'm not the only one who frustrates her.

"Mommy, we have to go," Alex says to Lydia, eagerly grabbing my hand to lead me in.

"Kisses first," she says and squats to shower his face with multiple kisses before letting him go.

"What about mine?" I tease, and she only rolls her eyes.

She holds my hand, kissing the back of my hand, "Watch over Alex."

I didn't expect that, so I can't help exchanging glances between her and my hand.

She bids us farewell, and I watch her leave.

My hand feels warm, almost like her lips are still pressed against it.

"Shall we?" I ask Alex as he leads me into the daycare.

It's fun. When was the last time I had this much fun? The kids are performing to celebrate the upcoming Father's Day, and the men are present. As I look around the room, I see men filled with gratitude; most of them are on the brink of tears from their children's performance.

As for me, I'm mesmerized.

After the performance, some of us read stories to the children, and I'm included. We have a little playtime with the kids, and I'm making a mental note to make some toy donations to this daycare. They seem fine, but a place dedicated to children should have more toys to keep them occupied.

I'll have James make the donation to be anonymous. I can't risk the teachers showing favoritism for Alex because of my donation.

Strangely, this will be the first time I'm doing something for charity that didn't involve some favoritism in return for my donation. Maybe I am changing a little bit too much.

The kids voluntarily talk about their fathers. To my surprise, all the kids chose to say something. I feel envious of all the other fathers present.

"Alex, do you have anything to say?" Mariam asks.

Well, we barely know each other, so Alex does not have much to say. Putting him on the spot might not be a good idea.

But despite my internal conflict, Alex nods, indicating he does have something to say.

I'm stunned.

"Uh. I don't have a dad," he says, and I can already feel the other fathers' confused stares, "But I have an Uncle Kevin. He plays with me, buys me toys and treats, then draws with me while mommy makes dinner."

I understand what he's saying, but I fear everyone else assumes that his mother and I are having an affair.

"I'm not sure what life is like with a dad," he continues, "But if it's like this, I don't mind having him as a dad."

The moment he mentions these words, everything around me stops. The only thing that continues to move is Alex tilting his head to the side, offering the most innocent smile.

I'm left with one thought. If only I had focused on my relationship with Lydia years ago, this beautiful boy would have granted me the honor of being my son...

Chapter 10

Let's Convince Your Mom

Kevin

"How did it go?" Lydia asks with a smirk, "And why are you grinning so much."

"I'm not grinning," I insist as I switch my facial expression to a frown, but as Alex tugs on my hand, it becomes difficult to keep up the facade.

Lydia grins and bursts into laughter.

"Mommy, Uncle Kevin read the story for us today," Alex reports to his mother, "Everyone loved it. I loved it, too!"

"Is that so?" She asks, then turns to me, "Why don't you read to us when we get home?"

"Don't push your luck," I frown as I walk past her.

"You don't want to read another story to me?" Alex asks with the saddest look on his face so far.

"What? No, I..." I try to apologize.

"Oh, how mean, how heartless," Lydia says in an overdramatic manner, hugging her son tightly while smirking at me, "And here I was thinking that he'd want to read to you privately tonight."

"Maybe he doesn't like reading stories," Alex says softly, sounding completely heartbroken.

It would be fine if it's just Lydia being dramatic, but I still can't stand seeing Alex sad.

"Fine, I'll read the story once we get home," I promise.

"Thank you, Uncle Kevin," he says, and I notice the mischievous smirk on his face, matching the one on his mother's face.

I roll my eyes in frustration, "Can I drive home?"

"Sure, why not?" Lydia agrees.

Strangely, she's acting completely different compared to this morning.

"Mr. Wills?" A man calls to my attention just as we're about to leave.

I recognize him, but I can't recall where we met besides at the daycare today.

"You don't remember, do you?" He chuckles softly. With some gray hair, a few wrinkles on his face, and dark suits, he's the grandfather of one of the kids at the daycare. Even with age catching up to him, he still looks like he can pass for a handsome, rich sugar daddy.

I take a look around and notice his security is not too far.

"Unfortunately, I don't," I admit, "I hope you won't mind reminding me where we met."

"Chicago. You helped my restaurant make an ad economically," he reminds me.

I blink twice, and then I remember him, "Mr. Roger Henry."

He nods with a smile, "Look at you. The twenty-year-old from almost two decades ago has completely grown up."

"Whatever you are doing to keep you looking this young, I want to know," I compliment him.

"Your tongue has remained the same," he says as he tries to contain his laughter. He pauses and turns his eyes to Alex and Lydia.

Alex is talking to his grandson with no care in the world, and Lydia has her eyes on them.

"I heard the news, and I'd like to apologize," he says.

"What?"

"Sandra Henry, she's my brother's daughter," he explains.

I glance sideways. What this man just said has also caught Lydia's attention, but she looks away.

"I see. It's a small world," I say with a dry chuckle.

"I understand the nervousness," he sighs, "I know Sandra is talented, but she can be a little spoiled. Her wild actions have made you abandon your post in New York." He pauses and returns his attention to Alex and Lydia, "Although I don't think it's a bad thing after all."

"What do you mean?" I frown.

"No need to be hostile," he says as he walks closer to me and whispers, "Maybe a family like this is what you need after all. I heard everything the boy said about you, so don't worry about the media finding out about your presence here today. I can make sure everyone stays quiet."

"Maybe it's because you're dressed in dark suits, and you look so serious, your statement sounds a little threatening. You're not hiring any hitman, are you?" I say to him, and he bursts into laughter, making me relax a little.

"You really are something else, aren't you?" He asks, "Well, you're trying to start a new life here. I'll help you out with ending the scandal to see if we can get you back to New York in time to bring your son to work."

"Oh, that activity, but the daycare says it's not required," I remind him.

"True, but you've already showed up to celebrate the upcoming Father's Day, haven't you? What happened to the arrogant businessman who always follows through with everything?" He asks.

"I think you're misunderstanding," I say as I raise my hand to stop him, "I'm just trying to help them out as a friend."

Did he think Lydia and I were together as a couple?

"I could have sworn," he mutters as he takes another look at Alex and Lydia, then a smile forms on his face, "Oh well, my vision might not be working as well as it used to."

"Grandpa, can Alex come to my birthday party next month?" Adrian, Roger's grandson, asks, interrupting our conversation.

"Sure, why not?" Roger agrees, then turns to me, "You are invited as well."

"I might be in New York then," I say to him.

"Up," Alex demands while stretching his hands towards me, and I pick him up.

"I won't be too quick to assume," he says as he turns to leave, "It's a pleasure seeing you again."

"Likewise," I reply as I watch him walk away.

"It's Malibu, after all, someone did recognize you. Mr. Secret Celebrity," Lydia says as she punches my arm playfully.

Is she cheering me up?

After our drive home and reading the story as I promised, we get ready for dinner.

Alex fell asleep, so it's just Lydia and I. It's a little hot, so I'm not wearing a shirt. Lydia has the same idea, wearing her sports bra to beat the heat.

I'm surprised to see it under her shirt, but she explains sometimes she prefers wearing sports bras, especially when she's working.

I'm helping to prep the ingredients, making mental notes of how I will start making my own meals when I return to New York.

Well, it might be too quick to assume I'll return to New York soon.

To be honest, I don't think I want to go back. My team is talented enough to run the company on their own without my input, so I can afford to stay an extra month for Roger's grandson's birthday party.

"I don't know if you noticed, but you stopped preparing the vegetables around five minutes ago," Lydia says, interrupting my thoughts.

"Oh, right," I resume shredding the carrots for the coleslaw.

"What's wrong?" She asks.

I sigh deeply, "I think you're right about me changing. It's still strange to me, but I haven't felt this much peace in a long time."

"Is that all?" She asks.

"That and, when I start thinking about everything I've done so far, the only emotions I'm left with are guilt," I answer.

"Shame?"

"Regret also," I add.

"I see," she remarks, "To think the once arrogant billionaire playboy will be vulnerable."

"Go ahead and laugh," I say, "It might help lighten the mood."

She turns her head and goes to stand behind me. I try to turn, but...

"Don't turn around," she demands. Her voice is a little shaky, but I must be thinking too hard about it.

I remain frozen, my eyes focused on the chopping board. I feel her fingers against my back, caressing gently.

"I'm not going to laugh at you," she says softly. Then I feel her body pressing against mine.

The sensation of her nipples pressing against my back tells me that she's taken off her sports bra.

"Lydia..." I call.

"Shh..." she silences me, "Just... stay still."

I do as she says. I still have no idea why she's doing this, but I have no complaints.

"You've been sending weird signals to me lately. I don't care if you've been doing it intentionally or not. I don't know if you've actually changed or if it's a temporary act until you return to New York," she starts to say as she moves her body in a circular motion, kissing my back and sending the heated sensation all over my body.

Her teeth against my shoulders aren't helping me, either.

"Alex.... He looked so happy today. Not just that, when you first spend time with him as a babysitter, I swear it looked so perfect," she continues, "I'm sure you're thinking that I'm acting like this as a way to thank you for what you've done for him. But it's only half true,"

She continues, "I'm grateful for you giving him a glimpse of what life with a father is like. And I appreciate you being so vulnerable." She pauses and starts kissing the back of my neck. I hold my breath from the overwhelming sensation, causing me to exhale sharply after several seconds.

"Lydia, you're trying to cheer me up, aren't you?" I ask with a warm smile.

"Call it Whatever you want," she says.

"You're really something," I say to her, and she kisses my back, hugging me tightly from behind.

"Let's get back to work," she says as she takes a step back, "I have to use the restroom."

"Thank you, though," I say to her.

"You don't have to thank me," she says before leaving.

She's a strange one, all right. She may be strict and straightforward, but she's finally warming up to me after all these years.

I've decided.

I'll get a little more serious about this relationship.

Chapter 11

Bring Your Kid To Work

Kevin

It's the weekend.

Lydia has both days off, and this Sunday is Father's Day. The daycare mentioned it wasn't required, but I want to take Alex to my office. I wouldn't want him to have anything to share with his friends when he goes back to the daycare on Monday.

As for my scandal, it's practically non-existent. Luckily, other celebrities seem to have more scandalous lives than mine, which helps my scandal disappear much faster. In fact, the media has moved on to the scandal of the famous celebrity couple, and I have a feeling that people don't even remember my incident with Sandra anymore.

James and the PR team have informed me that it's safe to return to the New York office but advised me to avoid public spaces.

Easy enough.

My private jet is ready to leave at any time, and so is Alex. I just need to convince Lydia to let it happen. When my old client, Roger, recognized me at the daycare, it was easily dismissible for her because it's Malibu, after all.

But this is New York, where the scandal started. Of course, I'm going to be careful, but it will take a lot of convincing to get her to come along.

"All right then, let's go," she says, agreeing immediately, leaving me with my mouth wide open.

Let me rewind a little.

It's Friday evening. I've made up my mind and am determined to convince Lydia to come to New York.

Dinner. A glass of wine for both of us and orange juice for Alex.

"Lydia, I'll be taking Alex with me to New York for the 'Bring Your Son To Work,'" I get straight to the point, "You'll be coming along with me as well."

"All right then, let's go," she agrees.

And we're back to the present.

"That's it?" I ask.

"You don't want me to agree?" She asks.

"I'm just surprised, that's all," I reply, "I expected a little resistance from you, thanks to the scandal and all."

"I'm worried about that, but everything seems to have calmed down," she explains, "I have a friend of mine who wouldn't shut up about your scandal before, but she hasn't said anything recently, so things are clear on that end. We just have to make sure we don't go anywhere where many people hang out."

I turn my attention to Alex, who has been listening to us with rapt attention. His eyes seem to say he has no idea what was discussed, but he fancies the idea of going to New York.

"Alex, have you ever been to New York?"' I ask.

Alex turns to his mother for permission, and she nods, giving the approval. Then he turns to me with a brighter smile, "No, I haven't. Are we really going there?"

"Yep, we are," I confirm with a warm smile.

Saturday.

The smell of New York City, the city of dreams... is polluted.

Maybe I've stayed in the Malibu hills for too long, and my lungs have gotten used to what fresh air smells like. Another reason why I don't think I want to return to this city in a hurry.

"That was fun," Alex says.

We're still at the private hangars after landing. Alex has never been inside an airplane before, so the flight with my private jet was his first experience. Boy, he was really excited during our flight to New York.

"We'll do it again tomorrow," I say to him, and he nods enthusiastically.

"The city of dreams, huh?" Lydia remarks as she looks around, "I've only been here twice. It's good to be back again."

"It doesn't smell polluted to you?" I ask.

"It seems like you've become accustomed to Malibu's fresh air. Do you miss the smell of the ocean and the trees on the hills already?"

"I do," I say, but I didn't think I'd be attached to Malibu this quickly.

"What are we waiting for?" Alex asks.

I'm about to answer, but the Rolls Royce starts to appear, and I say, "That," pointing to the car.

"Oh, nice!" The young man's eyes twinkle.

The car stops in front of us, and the driver steps out along with James. They are both excited to see me, but the confused look on their faces as they notice Lydia and Alex are priceless.

"Good morning, Gaston and James," I greet.

"Good morning, sir," they respond almost immediately.

"Good morning!" Alex greets enthusiastically.

His childlike innocence and adorable nature instantly steal both men's hearts, and they greet Alex.

"Gentlemen, meet Chef Lydia Johnson and her son, Alex Johnson," I start the introductions, "Lydia is the private chef from Peak Bites, and I asked them to accompany me."

"It's a pleasure to meet you," Lydia says, exuding an air of elegance.

It's my first time seeing her talk to people like that. *Oh wait, that's how she talked to me when we reunited.*

"Nice to meet you," James says, offering her a handshake, which she accepts, "I'm James, Mr Wills's assistant. Welcome to New York." After the handshake, he asks them to get in the vehicle and leave me alone with him.

Once they're in the car, he turns to look at me, "Excuse me, sir. What's going on?"

"What?" I raise a brow.

"Why are you here with your Chef and her son?" He asks.

"It's 'Bring Your Kid To Work' day," I reply in a matter-of-fact manner that makes his left brow twitch.

"You have a child?!" He asks, "Why am I hearing this now?"

"That's because I don't have a kid," I correct him, "Alex is here because I adore him in an uncle-nephew kind of way. And Lydia is here because... well, she's his mother."

"What's that look?" He asks while pointing at my face

"What look?"

"You haven't ever made a face like that," he says, "You're grinning. And it's not that same grin you usually have when we land major gigs." He lowers his voice, "Are you in love?"

"What? Don't tease me," I groan as I look to see Lydia in a car. Even with the tinted windows, I can feel Lydia's playful gaze.

"Wait. This.... This is good; we can use this to get the media off the Sandra case," James says.

"What?"

"I mean, if you show off your new love interest, and people see just how much you're in love, they'll be more interested in your new love life than the scandal with Sandra," he explains, "That way, everyone will..." he stops speaking as he notices the scowl on my face.

"We will not use Lydia or Alex for any media attention," I warn him.

He's startled. I've never been angry with him in all the years he's worked with me. In fact, if I were with another woman, I would have jumped on James' suggestion. Using relationships to get the media's attention is something the entertainment industry does often.

My talent agency would even advise an actor and an actress in a lead role to actually date to create a buzz. People want to see that dynamic on and off the screen.

James means no harm with the suggestion, and if the PR team finds out about Lydia and Alex, they would most likely suggest the same thing he suggested.

James is just doing his job as usual, yet it annoys me.

"I'm sorry for my outburst," I apologize, "I know you're trying to do your job, but we'll leave Lydia and Alex out of it. I plan to return to Malibu and continue my hiding out."

"You've changed," he says with a smile, "I guess your playboy era is coming to an end."

"What?"

"It's nothing," he shrugs, but the smile remains. He isn't offended by my response earlier, "Let's make sure Master Alex has a good time today."

Everyone's noticing my change, aren't they?

"Woah!!" Alex exclaims as he sees my office building.

It's only fifteen stories tall. But I guess kids are impressed easily.

Instinctively, I pick him up before he even asks me to carry him.

Lydia suppresses a chuckle. I turn and notice James is also holding back the urge to laugh. But neither of them seems to be mocking me.

"What?" I ask with a quizzical look.

"Oh, it's nothing," Lydia assures me. James nods in agreement.

"Let's go.., Uncle Kevin," Alex demands as he pulls on my cheek.

"Fine, fine," I groan as I make my way into the building.

The surprised look on my staff's faces is mildly entertaining in its own way.

I guess they didn't expect to see their boss arrive with a child.

But most of them are actually focused on Lydia.

She's wearing a white sundress and light makeup. Her hair isn't in a ponytail; she allows it to flow to her shoulders. She might be a bit short, but she seems to make it work for herself. The swaying of her hips, the way she purposefully tilts her head to acknowledge their staring, everything she does makes one assume two things.

One, she's a model who's here for a job.

Two, she's another fling the boss has brought to the office.

Knowing how perceptive she is, I can guess she already knows what's going through their minds as we walk around.

I put Alex down, and he brings out his notebook, ready to learn everything about what I do.

He follows closely behind James, who leads the tour, explaining what each department is in charge of.

Everyone easily falls in love with Alex at first sight, making the tour a little more fun for the young gentleman.

With his childlike charisma, I can easily see him becoming a decent, no, outstanding child actor. He's intelligent, adorable, and has a good voice.

Now that I think of it, my agency doesn't have any child actors besides the ones we employ for ads.

"I know that look," Lydia says as she flicks my shoulder.

"Ow," I flinch, "You do know most of my staff can see you."

"Should I be worried?" She asks.

"Aren't I supposed to be the arrogant one?" I murmur.

"I guess the influence is there," she shrugs, "What exactly were you thinking, looking at my son with those money-making eyes of yours."

"Don't you think Alex would be a good child actor?" I ask.

"I knew you were going to suggest that," she says with a sigh. Then, she turns her attention to Alex.

We're in the studio for photography, watching some models pose for a new product.

"Do you want to have your picture taken?" The photographer asks Alex, and he responds positively, "Good. Now go over there and strike a pose."

Alex gives me his notebook and pencil to hold as he makes his way to his stage.

He tries to mimic the poses the male model made earlier, and it's almost accurate.

Everyone present is surprised and some even start cheering for him. He has his pictures taken, and the photographer shows him the pictures.

"I see it," Lydia agrees with my earlier question.

"Sir," the photographer calls, "We might want to hire this boy."

I turn to look at Lydia, and I can see the pride for her son reflecting in her eyes, but she isn't too eager about it.

"Well, we might, but maybe when he's a little older," I say to him, "Lydia, do you mind if they use the pictures?"

"I don't mind," she says.

"All right then," I say and nod towards James.

"Mommy, did you see? I was a model," Alex says to her.

He takes his notebook and tries to write it down.

He spells '*model*' as '*mordell*'. Close enough.

'

We continue our tour, and he gets to meet with some actors he recognizes from some movies he's seen. Alex is having the time of his life, and I'm all for it.

We end the tour with my office, and I explain to him what my job entails: monitoring everyone else and representing the organization.

"If you're representing, then why aren't you here?" He asks.

James and Lydia visibly wince as he asks the question.

Of course, children have the tendency to ask whatever questions come to their mind.

"Long story," I say, as that's the only answer I can think of. "Don't worry, you'll understand when you're older."

The combination of these answers is as old as time, and it works.

I look at James and Lydia; neither seems satisfied with my answer.

You don't expect me to tell him the details of my scandal, do you?

They shrug as if they are reading my mind.

"Anyway, now that I'm here," I change the topic, "I should get some work done. Can you give me the status for all the projects?"

"Right, about the movie," James says.

Lydia gets seated as she helps with Alex's report about today's activity.

The sight of them working together gives me a smile and helps motivate me to work as well.

"And that's about it," James says with a sigh as we conclude for the day.

It's been two hours since the tour ended, and I've just finished catching up on everything.

Alex is just waking up after a nap.

"Sir, do you remember the amusement park not too far from here?" James asks in a whisper.

"Yeah? What about it?" I ask.

"Well, they are doing a special event there, and the tickets are currently discounted," he replies.

"I didn't know there was a promo like that. Did you get us an advertising gig from them?" I ask as I go back to review the files to see if I've missed anything.

"That's not what I was getting at," he says, turning his head to Lydia and Alex.

She is holding her son, who's trying to get his bearings while waking up from a nap.

"Oh," I realize what he meant, "Lydia, there's an amusement park nearby. Let's check it out."

Alex sits up, "With rollercoasters?!"

"Not until you're older, young man," I reply.

"Awww," his shoulders drop, but it's better than getting him on the roller coaster.

"Aren't you worried about the media?" Lydia asks.

"I think it's fine," James says, "There's always the option of renting out the entire place."

"I was about to suggest the same thing," I say in agreement.

"I'll inform the account manager," James says as he pulls out his phone to make the call.

"*Or,* you can wear a disguise," Lydia suggests, "Renting out the place will only make matters worse. Plus, no one will notice if you wear sunglasses and a baseball hat."

"Why do I have to hide my face?" I frown.

"Not too long ago, you didn't even get out of the house to be hidden from the media," she replies, "Just do this for me, okay?"

"Fine," I agree, "James, get me what she said."

"Thank you," Lydia says with a smile, "Could you get Alex and me sunglasses and hats also?"

"No problems," James says before leaving.

My phone buzzes, and I get a text from James; "*I never thought I'd see the day you would be willing to listen to a woman who wasn't your business partner.*"

Yeah, I never thought I would, either.

The amusement park is packed, and to be honest, the disguise only seems to make us stand out more.

I take off the sunglasses but leave the hat on. Alex and Lydia do the same.

We start exploring the park's attractions. The petting zoo is a favorite place for Alex and me. I've always wanted a pet, but I wasn't that responsible as a kid to have one, and too busy as an adult to get one.

We go to see a magic show, and Lydia is mesmerized. I'm surprised to see that she loves magic, to the point she volunteers to help on stage for the disappearing act.

As she returns, I can see the disappointment written on her face.

"What?" I ask.

"They don't actually make you teleport," she replies, "There was a false door, and the stage assistant asked me to pass through it."

"Wait, what? Did you actually think it was real?" I ask, trying to suppress the urge to laugh.

"It's not real magic?" Her eyes are wide open in shock, then her cheeks turn bright red as embarrassment takes over.

I can't hold it back anymore and burst into laughter.

"Stop laughing," she says while pouting and hitting my shoulder, "I knew it wasn't real."

It's still hard to believe that she actually believes in magic, but it makes her cuter than she already is.

I win some stuffed animals through the games, getting Lydia a carrot plushie and a shark one for Alex.

I wanted to just buy them at first, but I felt it was better to earn it.

Our last thing to do is the carousel. Alex rides with me, while Lydia rides the one next to us. I'll never forget this moment.

After a long day of having fun, I find a bench for us to sit down and relax while having our candy apples. Alex falls asleep almost immediately, and Lydia places her head against my shoulder.

"He's never going to forget today," she says.

"And neither am I," I assure her.

"Hmm....thank you," she says, "For helping create fond memories..."

With a side glance, I notice her falling asleep.

I'm not sleepy in the slightest, so it's fine to keep watch over them.

A family walks past us, the father carrying his sleeping child. As he sees me, a smirk forms on his face, "Show off." I want to explain that it's not my family, but I just let it be.

"That was the most beautiful date you've been in," James says as he walks up to me.

I was already aware he had been watching us all this time.

"Are you ready to leave?" He asks, "The car is ready."

"Ten more minutes," I answer.

Chapter 12

Just This Once

Lydia

Bliss. I can't really deny it any longer. I try to avoid falling in love with him again, but it's not working.

Kevin. He's changed. I can't deny it. It's for real. His arrogance is nothing more than a facade now, as he only uses it when I tease him.

When we first reunited, I had nothing but disdain for him. But only a few days later, I was slowly warming up to him again. Watching him bond with Alex only increased my desire for him.

Little by little, he's torn down the wall of defense I've spent years building to avoid men like what he used to be.

When he held my nape and kissed my neck, he gave me a chance to escape, so I can't say I was trapped. When he tried to move away, I found myself stretching towards him again.

When he showed me his vulnerable moment, I wanted to console him. I wish it were my only excuse, but seeing him shirtless wasn't exactly helping me think properly. I imagined his fingers and mouth dominating the sweet spot between my legs.

Something about him just exudes a kind of peace he didn't possess eight years ago.

Little by little, I've started letting down my guard around him. I'm sure he's already noticed, and I can tell if it were the old him, he'd have taken advantage of me easily.

But he hasn't.

I'm not going to lie, but maybe he really hasn't noticed me because I'm a mother now. I'm falling asleep on his shoulder, and perhaps I'm already dreaming, but I feel like I'm being carried by him. I remember opening my eyes and seeing his face. I was still feeling drowsy, half asleep, but I could tell where we were moving.

I wake up in a bed with Alex sleeping next to me. His mansion here in New York is much bigger and more impressive than his house in Malibu.

It takes me a while to orient myself in the new environment.

I find him in the living room with the TV on, and yet, he's going through Alex's notes for today with the biggest smile on his face. He is dressed in a comfortable cotton T-shirt and shorts, holding a cup of beverage in one hand. He takes a sip from a cup and returns the cup to the coffee table without losing focus on Alex's note.

He doesn't notice me as he flips through the pages. It's easy to tell he's recalling the events from today, and I don't want to interrupt him. But at the same time, I've become addicted to teasing him.

"Did you enjoy today that much?" I ask, disrupting his thoughts.

He lifts his head slowly, and I'm probably hallucinating again because he looks so hot in a casual T-shirt and shorts.

"I actually did," he replies with a smirk, "I didn't think I would ever meet an adult who didn't know how magic works."

"I said, I know how it works!" I insist. The embarrassment from recalling the memory makes my face bright red again.

"You're so adorable," he smiles and motions for me to come closer with his left index finger.

I obey and make my way to him. I remember him doing something like this to me years ago. If I got any closer, he'd make me sit on his thighs.

Okay, now I'm excited.

"But he taps the chair's arm on the couch for me to sit."

My excitement disappears, and I take my seat where I am instructed to. I'm not happy about it.

"You know, sometimes I forget he's only four years old," he remarks as the grin returns to his face, "So intelligent. His mother's genes are definitely at work."

"You could just praise me directly, you know?" I say to him.

"And risk you getting an even bigger head than you already have? Not a chance," he replies without even looking at me.

His impudence earns him a flick to the side of his temple.

"Hmph," he pouts as he gives me a side-eye.

"Don't give me that look," I say, "You're the one who is being mean."

"You say mean things, too, you know?" He reminds me.

"Me? Never!" I feign ignorance.

"I give up," he sighs in defeat, "You win."

"As I should," I say with a smug look, and he just chuckles gleefully before turning his attention to the book.

It's the first time I've heard him laugh so playfully.

"You have a beautiful laughter," I remark.

"Thank you," he says, "Every expression of yours is beautiful."

"You're only teasing me," I sigh.

"I wish I was," he mutters softly.

"What?"

"Hmmm? No, I didn't say anything," he says.

His statement actually made my heart skip a beat.

"Mom? Uncle Kevin?" Alex calls while yawning, "I'm hungry."

"Are your chefs around?" I ask Kevin.

"I dismissed them for today," he replies, "I'm making spaghetti and meatballs. Already done with the sauce and meatballs. Just getting the water boiled to cook spaghetti."

"I'm impressed," I say, "You're actually going out of your way to cook. I have to pinch myself. Am I dreaming now?"

Alex makes his way to Kevin and snuggles into his lap, drifting off into sleep again.

I'm jealous of my son.

"I don't think I can cook in this situation," he says.

"Just the pasta left, right?" I ask as I get up.

"Thank you for the help," he says.

I've made dinner, and Alex is awake again but still sleepy, so Kevin helps feed him.

After dinner, I take my son and change him into his PJs before tucking him into bed.

It's my turn to change out of the sundress.

After taking off my dress, I stare at myself in the mirror.

My abs are still flat, and my boobs and hips that have gotten bigger. I'd say I've taken care of myself pretty well to look good.

I know I'm not supposed to be reading too much into it, but why does Kevin ignore every chance he has to be with me?

Oh, no... What am I talking about?

I sigh and switch into what I brought as my nightwear - simple pajama shorts and a camisole.

I better go thank him for his hospitality and today's activities.

I'm not able to find him in the living room, so I try to navigate my way to his bedroom.

I knock on the door.

"Come in," his voice reaches me from behind the door.

I open it and find him on the bed; the lights are on, and he's reading a book. He lifts his eyes, and I can feel them settle on my body before making their way back to my face.

I should have come over here while I was still wearing the dress.

"Are you okay? Is the bed comfortable? Is Alex tucked in?" It seems like he is trying to get control of the situation at hand by the series of questions.

I come and close the door behind me, "Everything is okay. Can I sit next to you?"

"Sure," he replies.

I make my way to the bed and sit by his side, "Of course, your bed is really hard. What's your body made of?"

"Marble," he replies jokingly, "That explains this sculpted body, doesn't it?"

"Keep telling yourself that," I sigh. I must admit he's not lying about his sculpted body.

On the way to his bedroom, I found one room with a lot of gym equipment. I bet he works out a lot to keep his physique at the top level.

"What are you reading?" I ask as I take a peak into the book.

"Cooking for dummies," he replies and shows me the cover to prove it, "I don't think I got the meatballs right today, so I want to improve. Maybe I can help you lessen the workload a little."

"You're making it sound like you want me to cook for you forever," I tease.

"That doesn't sound so bad, does it?" He asks, turning his face to me.

He's too close. Laying by his side wasn't a good idea...

My heart is pounding again.

Quick, think of something else.

"I uh.... I came to thank you..." I start to say, but his face keeps getting closer.

He doesn't have me pinned down, so I can leave if I want to.

I can't move. Well, it's more like I *won't* move.

"Today was a good..."

He's closer; I can feel him. My head is tilting, vision dimming.

Our lips make contact. His lips rub against mine softly, then pull back.

I open my eyes, and he's still staring at me; he's holding back, giving me a chance to let him stop.

I can do just that. I can get up and return to my room, and we can act like nothing happened by tomorrow morning.

That's another option, but my body and spirit are too weak to follow the above options.

I take the charge and kiss him hungrily. He groans with relief and holds my hips, making me sit on him.

I continue to consume his lips like it's my first time kissing someone. It's clumsy, hurried, and rushed, but he doesn't complain, receiving my frustrations.

As he holds my nape, he starts to kiss back, giving me a proper kiss.

His left hand holds my nape in place, his right hand secures my hip, and then he offers his tongue, gently tangling with mine. His tongue is big, and as he feeds me with it, I'm gasping for air while sucking on it.

Then I feel *it*.

His dick is rising against his pants and poking at me for my attention.

"What's this?" I ask with a dazed look, drunk with his kiss and intoxicated by my own sexual urges.

"Ignore it," he replies.

"But it hurts, doesn't it?" I ask him.

"You're something else," he says as he casually pulls down my camisole, revealing my breasts.

At first, I hunch a little and cover them. But Kevin holds my arm and moves it out of the way, "Let me see your body, Lydia."

His words stir me, so I sit upright and force my chest out for him to see. My nipples are already aching for him. Both are harder than when I rubbed them against his back.

He cups them in his hands, then lifts the right one to his mouth.

The wetness of his mouth and the ferocious flicking of his tongue against my nipple is a sensation I have long forgotten.

As he sucks, other parts of my body start to throb for him. I've managed to remain celibate for years, only relieving myself with toys, but there's nothing that beats the real thing.

ARROGANT BILLIONAIRE'S DO-OVER

He switches to my left breast while driving his thumb into my right nipple, stirring it as hard and fast as he can. The sensation has me muffling my moans.

More.... I want more.

As he stops sucking, I gasp, trying to catch my breath. I stare at my breasts shining with his saliva.

"What's with the face?" He asks with a wicked smile, "Oh well, I guess that's all for tonight."

He actually means it. I know he wants more; the throbbing of his dick has been calling out to me the whole time.

In my case, my pussy is already calling as well.

"No... that's not all for tonight," I manage to say while panting.

"Are you sure? We can stop here," he gives me the chance to escape.

"No... just this once," I insist.

I can deal with everything else in the morning, but right now, we both need to take care of our desires.

"If you insist," he says, "But it's your turn."

I nod in agreement and kiss his neck as I start undoing his buttons, pushing the shirt away from his body. I use my tongue to circle around his nipple; his gentle groan of satisfaction is enough to motivate me to continue.

I go lower, pulling on his pants. He's nacked, so I have to be too.

I pull down my shorts, leaving only the camisole on my waist. Using my right index and middle finger, I start rubbing against my pussy, while stroking his dick with my left.

His seven inches worth of meat already had me panicking already as I imagined how it would fit in my mouth or pussy.

I kiss the tip gently, then lick from the base to the underside of his tip. The scent of his dick is driving me crazy in a good way. My pussy is already dripping, and I'm yet to have him in my mouth.

I make eye contact with him, and he's staring at me with his lips slightly ajar and sharp breathing. I'm doing a good job. Then I place him in my mouth, and his body jerks in response.

Sucking only on his tip and he holds my head, "Lydia, stop... it's sensitive."

I'm not listening and continue to torture him. He holds back and tries to lift his hips to put the rest of him in my mouth, but I keep moving my head back.

So, rather than holding my head in place, he forces my head down, and his length expands my mouth. While I'm still taken aback, he grabs my head tightly and starts to move my head up and down along his length, fucking my mouth with the intent to punish such a naughty girl.

I can't breathe, and I'm on the verge of gagging. He stops and pulls out, letting me catch my breath.

"You had enough?" He asks with a smirk.

I smirk in response, "Coward."

ARROGANT BILLIONAIRE'S DO-OVER

"Agreed, now turn around," he commands.

I obey and turn around, instinctively stretching into the cat pose. It's an embarrassing pose, but here I am, going crazy with the anticipation. Even with my last lover, it was my favorite position.

He holds my thighs, and I can feel his breath against my pussy, and he even blows air against it, further exciting me.

Then his lips come in contact, and he starts to eat my wet pussy slowly but intensively. He captures my clits, and I cling to the bedsheets for support. His tongue flicking against my clit and alternating between sucking and licking is making me wild.

"Oh my god..." I'm panting and moaning; my hips seem to have developed a mind of their own as they start to move against his face. I don't need a mirror to show me the intense pleasure expressed on my face.

He stops sucking, and his right hand holds down my right thigh. I can feel his fingers start rubbing against my slit. I know what he's thinking. The size of his fingers makes my slit look too small.

"How many can you take?" He asks.

"One..., two..." I'm not sure, but I think I can handle that.

He slides in one finger, and I'm a little tight, mostly because I can't relax.

"Relax, Lydia," he says softly as he kisses my back.

"Oh...," I reply and try to relax my breathing, loosening up a little for him.

Then he shoves the second finger quickly, "Aww...," I groan in pleasure as his fingers explore my insides until he finds my g-spot. As he finds the sweet spot, he presses down against it, his thumb remains outside, rubbing against my clit.

This is just foreplay, and I'm already getting close to climaxing. The gradual increase of his pace in me has me moaning out loud.

"Shh...." He hushes me as he stops moving his fingers, "Any more sounds, and I'll have to stop entirely. Is that what you want?"

Don't make a single sound? Is he out of his mind?

"Is that what you want?" He repeats the question as he starts pulling out his fingers slowly.

"No, please," I beg, "I'll be quiet, I promise."

Why do I feel like I've just set myself up for a disaster?

Chapter 13

What Happens Next?

Lydia

"Good girl," he says and pulls out his fingers.

I turn to look at him, completely confused. *I promised I wouldn't make any more noise, didn't I?*

He's licking his fingers as if it's the best thing he's ever tasted.

"Lovely," he praises, "On your back, hold your legs up."

I obey immediately, turning to lay on my back and raising my legs for him.

He lets out a menacing chuckle, "Isn't this quite the sight?"

Using the fingers that had just been inside me, he rubs them against my lips, "Open."

I open my mouth and let his fingers in.

"You are surprisingly obedient tonight," he remarks, "Where are all the snarky remarks and the teasing you are so fond of?"

I can't answer. His questions are only making me feel a little dirty and hot. I don't think I want to admit it, but I'm enjoying it.

"No answer?" He raises his brow, then brings his cock towards my pussy, rubbing his tip against my clit and entrance, "Will this fit?"

That better be a rhetorical question because I'm too far gone to have him stop because of its size.

He places the tip and tries to insert it. It hurts a bit at first, but not too much to be a problem. He places his hand on my belly and urges me to relax and trust him. I take in a deep breath to let myself calm down.

He moves, and I can finally feel him inside my body.

"All right, just a little more to go, or are you okay with this length?" He asks.

What? Is he only halfway in?

I look down, and he's not joking.

"I can't take anymore," I admit.

"It's okay, this will be enough," he assures me, "Ready?"

As soon as I nod, he starts moving. I can feel my insides loosen up as he thrusts in and tightens again as he pulls out, almost like it was responding to his body.

I have never felt anything like this before.

He places my legs on his shoulders and slowly moves the rest of his length into me.

"God... you feel so good, Lydia," he praises.

"Kisses," I ask.

"So adorable," he teases and leans forward to kiss me.

I can't get enough of this.

His kisses, accompanied by the gentle movements of his hips, are heavenly.

I hope I don't become addicted to this.

"Faster, please," I plead as soon as my body has gotten used to his size and its movements.

He starts to move faster and deeper, each thrust hitting against my cervix with every intention of going into my womb. Everything in me starts to shake, thanks to his furious pounding.

"Awww... I can't... hold it, please..." I plead, remembering his deal not to make any noise.

There's no way I can keep my voice down when I'm feeling something this good. My body is melting from the pleasure, and it's going wild.

"You're desperate, aren't you?" He asks in his husky voice, which makes me feel so small, "Fine, you don't have to be quiet."

I embrace him, letting him take control of my body as he deems fit.

"You should see the face you're making right now," he says as he pulls.

My pussy is gaping, and it's taking a little while to close, but I'm not completely satisfied.

He leads me to the full body mirror for me to look at myself.

My nipples are still hard, my face looks flushed, and my thighs – soaking with my honey.

I'm a mess. I really look like a mess.

"You look beautiful," he says as he stands behind me.

The difference in our heights and bodies makes me feel small. Has he always been this big?

I look in the mirror and notice his cock is still throbbing. I'm still shocked that something that massive was inside me a few seconds ago.

He holds my hip with one hand, and then the other holds down my head, bringing it closer to the mirror.

"You don't have to look away," he says, "I want you to see the kind of face you make when drowned in pleasure."

He shoves his dick into me again.

The first thing I notice in the mirror is how he lifts his head slightly when he's in me and how wide my mouth is open. He holds my breasts tight to support himself, and he's squeezing my nipples, also.

Then he starts to move again.

Compared to when we were in bed, his thrusts are now shorter, quicker, and more powerful.

My entire body jerks with each thrust. I bite my lower lip as I focus on the image in the mirror.

It must be my imagination, but he's getting bigger while I'm getting smaller. With the way his muscles contract, while he makes love to me, it feels like watching a wolf sexually devouring a bunny.

It's weird, but I love it with Kevin. If this were with anyone else, I would have hated it.

Kevin, who's become more like a father figure to my son.

Kevin, who praises my skills.

Kevin, who's making an effort to change his life.

Kevin, who eyes my body with lust but respects my desires.

Kevin, Kevin, Kevin...

"I'm right here," he says as he grabs my hair, pulling me to himself, "I'm not running anywhere, Lydia."

Somewhere along my thoughts, I was moaning his name.

Yeah, I'm definitely losing my mind.

He lifts my right leg, supporting it under his arm.

"I think the mirror has seen enough of you," he says in a jealous tone, "It's my turn."

He holds my chin, kissing me deeply, but it doesn't stop him from moving.

It's too much, and yet I can't get enough. I'm getting close.

"Lydia... I'm getting close," he warns.

"Just a little more, keep going," I demand.

And he maintains the pace, hitting against the spot that's causing me to reach my pleasure.

"Lydia...," he calls, and this time it almost sounds like a whisper.

"Call me again... but don't stop... please."

"Lydia... Lydia... Lydia..."

"Yes... that's me... I'm here..."

Judging by how his cock pulsing so much in me, I can tell he's really fighting back the urge to cum.

"Almost there..." I moan, and finally, I get the release, digging my nails into his arms.

"Aww...." He groans as he pulls out.

I quickly get on my knees, grab his dick and stroke him while his groans get louder and deeper.

"Oh..., Fuck...," he moans as he shudders, with my hand focused on his tip, trying to get every last drop out of him.

"Uh..." I exclaim while I enjoy the after-sensation of my orgasm while watching Kevin come. He's still semi-hard, but I'm sure he's had enough. Anything more would kill us both.

I place my hand against my pussy, and it feels a little stickier than usual.

I guess he couldn't pull out in time, thanks to me.

As we cuddle into bed, I'm staring at the ceiling.

He's still awake.

"My sister is coming in tomorrow, so Alex and I will have to leave," I interrupt the silence, "As the scandal has almost settled down," I pause before asking the question, "Will you remain in New York?"

"I have some things to review in the office tomorrow, but I'm returning to Malibu," he replies.

"Oh, why? Is something happening in Malibu?" I ask.

"Alex has to attend Adrian's birthday party," he answers, "I have to be there."

There he goes, hiding his true feelings, but his answer makes me happy. I can't really blame him for hiding his true feelings because I'm still hiding mine.

"The sex. It was wonderful." I tell him, looking into his eyes.

"Yeah, it was," he says, "So why did you do it?"

"I can ask you the same question," I sigh.

"You're a weird one," he teases.

"Says you," I tease in return, and we both chuckle softly, "It's still a one-time thing, though," I say.

"I know." He nods.

But we both know I'm lying.

"Will Alex look for you when he wakes up?" He asks.

"I just have to wake up earlier," I answer, snuggling into his arm.

I'm starting to fall asleep while he strokes my hair gently. His heartbeat acts as a lullaby to aid the process. As we drift into sleep, we seem to have the same question in mind, *"What happens next?"*

CHAPTER 14

What Happened To You?

Kevin

Even in my sleep, I can tell someone's in my bed. The stirring causes me to open my eyes.

And there she is – sitting at the corner of the bed, trying to put on the clothes she had on before coming to my room last night.

Last night.

I remember it. I can still feel it.

She is humming the gentle tune as she gets ready. She gets to her feet and turns her attention toward the bed, and all I can do is stare lovingly. She is glowing.

I'm still lost in thought, and I don't notice she is leaning close to my face. By the time I realize, her face is right in front of mine.

I'm startled, and it makes her grin.

"Good morning," her voice is as gentle as a feather caressing a cheek.

"Good morning," my voice is raspier than usual, but it seems that hearing my voice excites her visibly.

"I thought you'd sleep a little longer," she admits, pulling her face away, "What made you wake up earlier?"

I couldn't feel you next to me. There's no way I'm telling her that.

"I usually wake up around this time," I answer.

"Mm-hmm," she nods, "I'll go check on Adam. Hopefully, he isn't awake yet."

I sit upright, but my whole body still feels stiff from waking up. Thanks to Lydia, my morning erection is more sturdier than usual.

I didn't notice it last night, but her camisole hugs her body tightly, and her breasts fill out nicely. Her nipples are visible through the fabric shielding them.

Years ago, I didn't get to see her completely naked, but she was dressed in similar ways. The shorts she wore also concealed a part of her beautiful thighs.

She eyes me, and her gaze lowers to my crotch.

A smug look on her face, "Didn't I tell you it was only going to be a one-time thing?"

"Don't flatter yourself," I smirk, "This is just a natural phenomenon. It's a man thing."

"Really? It has nothing to do with me at all?" She inquires as she returns to bed, her head between my legs.

I swallow hard. It's too late for me to deny or confirm her inquiry.

Her fingers delicately trace a line against my bulge, and then she cups the bulge, blowing warm air directly against it.

"Aren't you going to say anything?" She asks with a shaky breath as she pulls my underwear, revealing my length.

She exhales sharply as she places my rod against her face, a smile on her face as she kisses the tip, causing me to throb eagerly, waiting to see what else she can do.

"You like that, don't you?" She asks, "What's that you said earlier? About your erection not having anything to do with me?"

Before I can answer, she places my member in her mouth, swallowing my length down to my base. I pause to breathe, allowing myself to indulge in the wetness and warmth of her mouth.

She pulls back and swallows again. Each time she moves around, I lose more control, lost in ecstasy.

"Mmm..." I groan as she continues to consume me, and I can't do anything to stop her.

She starts to move her head faster. Her eyes hold my gaze. The glint in her eyes tells me she's enjoying seeing me in a tormented state.

It's getting close. I'm almost there.

My breathing is rushed, and my abs clenches.... Just a little more.

Then she stops suddenly. My eyes widen in shock.

"And that's all," she says as she gets down from the bed, leaving my dick throbbing painfully in protest. My climax is already at the base of my hardness, and she stops like it means nothing to her.

"What do you mean that's all?" I frown.

"It has nothing to do with me, remember?" She grins, "Don't worry, you can handle it yourself while I wake up, Alex."

I can't complain or do anything but watch her leave the room, her hips swaying sensually. As she gets to the door, she gives me a dirty look before leaving me alone with a throbbing dick.

"That woman," I sigh and hold my member, stroking my dick slowly.

"You're not coming back?" Alex asks.

We're at my private hangar, where the jet is waiting to take Lydia and Alex home.

"I'll be there soon. I just need to take care of some things here," I promise him.

He doesn't buy it, and I can see signs of tears brimming.

"Alex, don't cry," I squat to be on the same level as him, "I promise you that I'll be back immediately after I'm done."

"Okay," he sniffles and embraces me.

I embrace him as well, absorbing his childlike warmth.

This is bad, and I'm starting to see him as my son.

I can feel the stares coming from James and Lydia, so I let go of Alex and face the two adults wearing stupid grins on their faces.

"Wipe that look off your faces," I roll my eyes.

"Don't keep us waiting too long, Kevin," Lydia says as she walks past me, leading Alex to the jet. She pauses and turns to look at me, "I mean it."

I don't know what she means by that, but it fills me with excitement.

Waiting until she and Alex have taken off, I head back to the office.

"So, while she's already making plans to have a public apology, I still think we should sue Sandra," one of the PR team members suggests.

We're trying to figure out what to do about Sandra's case. At least *they* are.

For me, my mind is somewhere else - back in bed, with a stubborn beauty lying next to me—the same beauty who teased me with my shaft in her mouth this morning.

I miss her already.

Have they arrived safely? Should I call? I should call her.

"Sir?" James calls.

I lift my head and notice my team is staring at me.

"What?" I blink twice.

"We were saying we might have to sue Sandra," Stella, the head of PR, repeats herself, "But James says there's no need as you can return to New York once she makes a formal apology."

"Oh, I see," I respond.

They're quiet, exchanging glances with each other.

"Uh..., what do you think, sir?" Stella asks, "You're the victim here. We need to know what you think."

"Just let her apologize," I reply, "She's been a wonderful talent to us. We can't let something like this ruin our relationship. We might need her for more roles in the future."

I'm done with my suggestion, and the rest of them are looking at me with surprised expressions.

"Stop looking at me like that!" I growl, "What did I say this time?"

"Much better," Stella lets out a sigh of relief, "We're just surprised because we remember you were swearing to bring her down before, so it's a nice surprise to see you've calmed down."

"What do you guys think I am? Some grumpy rich guy?" I ask.

They stare at each other and nod positively.

"I mean, it's been part of your character tropes for this incident," another team member points out.

"I see. That's how you guys see me..." I roll my eyes and reach for my phone, "Is the meeting done?"

"Yes, that's basically it. We already have everything under control," Stella replies, "Also, good news, you can stay in New York now. We've missed having you around."

"Save your flattery," I say, "You have done even better than when I was not around here in the office. Maybe I should let you guys handle things on your own for a while, and I'll return to Malibu."

"I don't think so," Stella says.

"All right, that's enough for today," James says as he gets up, "Meeting adjourned. Go out there and work on your tasks to do, and let's focus on hitting our annual company targets."

They all get up and start leaving one after the other until my assistant, James, and I are left alone.

"You seem very eager to go back there," James grins, "Could it be that Lydia has finally captured your heart?"

"It's nothing like that," I respond. "I promised Alex I'd be back soon. What kind of a man breaks the promise and breaks his heart?"

"What kind of a man denies what his heart truly wants?" He makes a smart comment.

"What?" I raise a brow.

"Oh, it's nothing," he sighs, "I understand your urgent desire to get back to Malibu, but we would really love your presence here. At least to motivate the staff."

He explains, "Most of them were really worried about you as it's the first time you're facing a scandal. Just give them your presence temporarily, and then you can return to your family."

"They are not..." I sigh, "Fine. I apologize."

"I also don't know what Lydia did to you, but you've become rather tame," he remarks with a smirk, "We kind of miss the grump who rarely listens to anyone."

"I haven't changed," I assure him.

"Sure," he says as he gets up to leave.

I dial Lydia's number.

Chapter 15

The Trouble Is Coming

Lydia

We're back in Malibu.

The short trip to New York was excellent, and Alex loved being on a plane where he didn't have to sit in place and got the opportunity to run around as much as he wanted.

"Go change your clothes," I say to him as we enter the house.

He's wearing a T-shirt that Kevin got for him.

He doesn't want to take it off. At least, that's what his pouting expression seems to say.

"You don't want to take it off?" I ask.

"Uncle Kevin gave me this," he answers, reminding me as if I've forgotten about it.

"Fine, but take off the shoes," I say to him.

"Okay, mummy!" He beams with smiles as he leaves his room.

I sink into the sofa and let out a sigh.

As I finally relax, my body starts to remember everything. The image in the mirror as my face flushes from the intense pleasure. The sensation of having his member inside me, hitting the right spots. The sound of his groans as he came.

He dominated me in his bedroom.

I eye the stairs; Alex may be coming downstairs soon.

Should I please myself? I shake off the thought and try to relax.

Thinking about something else might help. Let's see.

He took us to the amusement park, and we spent time together. He didn't have to do it, but he did and gave Alex and me a wonderful time. When was the last time I saw Alex having so much fun?

I spent most of my time caring for him with the mindset that we wouldn't need a father figure in his life. I didn't expect that if anyone were going to be a father figure for my son, it would be Kevin, the man who cared about only himself.

The arrogant billionaire playboy who was never ready to settle down.

The man I dated many years ago and never mentioned wanting to start a family.

The man who told me that he didn't want to commit to our relationship because his career or his playboy image was more important than starting a family.

The man I was forced to reunite with because of my job.

I promised myself that I would keep our relationship professional and avoid him, but he just seemed to find a way into my heart with little to no effort.

"And I miss him already," I sigh.

I stare at my phone for a moment, considering if I should call him to tell Alex and I had arrived safely or not bother him at all.

While I continue to go back and forth, the phone starts to ring.

The caller ID shows it's him.

My heart starts racing just from a phone call.

Then again, this is Kevin. He never bothered to call to see if I had gotten home safely when we were dating eight years ago.

I answer the phone, "It seems like you couldn't handle a day without me."

"I wasn't expecting you to answer," he replies.

"What? Why?"

"I don't know," he says, "For some odd reason, I feel nervous..."

"You? nervous?" I raise a brow, "Knowing you, I never thought there would be a time I would hear you say nervous."

"You really are changing," I add.

"And you and Alex are to blame for it," he whispers.

"What was that?" I ask.

"It's nothing," he brushes it off, "Have you guys arrived safely?"

"Yes, we arrived safely just a few minutes ago. Thank you," I respond with gratitude, "Is everything going well in the office?"

"Everything is going well. Maybe I should retire early," he replies.

"And do what then?"

"Maybe go to Malibu and have you work for me for the rest of your life."

It makes my heart skip a beat, but I brushed it off, "Sounds like hell to me."

"Of course it would," he chuckled, "Last time I checked, I don't like seeing you at peace."

"And I don't like seeing you at peace, either," I smirk.

We laugh, and there's a comfortable silence as we settle.

I can't stop thinking about last night. The question I had in mind comes back to haunt me again.

What next?

"Lydia?" He calls.

"Yes?" I answer immediately.

I can hear him swallow and his breathing labors. He's having a hard time spitting out the words he has to say.

"Do you...." He finally finds the courage, but the following words are silent, and I can barely hear them, "... Maybe try... again."

"What did you..." my words are cut short by the sound of tiny feet scrambling towards me.

"Mom, is Auntie still coming over?" Alex asks, interrupting the moment.

"Sweetie, I'm on the phone," I reply.

"Okay," he says and sits on the floor to wait.

"I'm sorry, Kevin. What were you saying?" I return my attention to him, trying to figure out what exactly he meant.

"Is that Uncle Kevin? Let me say hi!" Alex tugs at my pants.

"Oh, let me speak to him," Kevin says. It's a perfect opportunity to let him change the topic.

"But I thought..." it's no use, "fine, I'll give it to him."

I hand the phone over to my excited son, placing it on a speaker.

"Hi, Uncle Kevin," my little boy greets with excitement.

"Hey Alex," Kevin returns the greeting, and I can picture him wearing a huge smile, "How was your trip back? Did you have fun?"

"I did. We were the only ones in the plane," Alex reports like it's a big deal, "And we were so high up in the air!"

"That does sound like fun," Kevin remarks.

"You should have come with us," Alex pouts.

"I know. But I have work to do," Kevin sighs, "But don't worry. When I return, we'll think of something fun to do together, okay?"

"Yay," Alex giggles and returns the phone to me.

"All right. Get going," I instruct my little guy, then focusing on Kevin, "You were.... trying to tell me something."

"Oh, it's nothing. Never mind," he says.

"Sir, we need your input on something," James says in the background.

"Take good care of Alex," Kevin instructs, "I'll be with you guys soon."

I'm really disappointed as I still want to know what he was trying to tell me, but I let it go.

"All right," I sigh, "thank you for the wonderful time in New York."

"You're welcome."

As the call, I'm left to my thoughts again, but they are now in disarray.

Two Days Later.

I've been occupied with trying to catch up with my work at Peak Bites and everything else at home. My sister has been caring for Alex, allowing me to focus on work.

I don't know what happened, but most of my colleagues seem harsher than usual. It's easy to tell my time is coming to an end.

"What exactly happened when I was gone?" I ask Allison over the phone.

It's the end of the workday, and I'm trying to get Alex ready for bed. We were busy at the restaurant today, so Allison and I could not talk.

"Oh, nothing serious," she replies, "the mayor came around and wanted to give another contract. He saw you weren't on duty and decided to wait until you got back because he wanted your input."

"Why would he do that?" I ask, trying not to raise my voice, "Does he want to put me out of a job?"

"I don't think you'll have any problem finding a job right away if the boss sacks you," she says, "but the boss wasn't too pleased. And a lot of the staff agree with him."

"Oh, fuck," I groan.

"It's all right. I'll get you fired quickly, so you don't have to worry about what the staff says about you anymore," Allison teases.

"Get lost," I chuckle softly.

There's a knock on my door, followed by the sound of a doorbell.

"Hold on, I seem to have a visitor," I tell her.

"A visitor? It's past eight p.m., and you never have visitors that late," she states.

She's not wrong—anyone who wants to see me that late would usually call ahead of time.

Is it Kevin?

The last time we had a chance to talk to each other was two days ago. He has his hands full trying to grow his business, and I hear his agency got another big contract. So, I'm not expecting him back anytime soon.

"Could it be the mayor?" Allison asks.

"It better not be," I reply.

The ringing and knocking continue, but it's not aggressive. As I approach the door, I can't help feeling something is wrong.

Then I hear his voice, "Lydia, it's me."

Just those three words, and I can feel my anger rising. The second source of all my problems is at the door. He has the nerve to finally show himself up after all these years. Unbelievable!

Worried that he might try something, I go upstairs to get my pepper spray.

I'm not letting him back in my life ever again.

Chapter 16

Something Happened

Kevin

Things have been going well. The case with Sandra is finally over, at least on the surface. The movie deal I had been chasing is finally signed and ready to go. There is no bad blood between Sandra and me anymore, so we offered her a role in this project.

"I'm really sorry about all this," Sandra apologizes for the thirteenth time.

"It's okay, you don't have to apologize anymore," I tell her.

"It's just...." She says, "I couldn't help my feelings for you. I know what we had was purely physical, but I thought maybe something more than physical would blossom from it."

I don't say anything and allow her to continue.

"But it seems like you can't even look at me anymore," she adds, "do you hate me?"

"If I hated you, I wouldn't have offered you the role in this project," I reply, "I have forgiven you. In fact, I think I even understand why you did it. So I'm not mad at you anymore."

"You... you seem different," Sandra says with an evident look of surprise, "What happened to you?"

"Everyone keeps saying that," I sigh, "I'm still the same person."

She continues to stare at me. James is in the office as we discuss, but he's pouring himself a shot of my whiskey.

"Kevin, did you fall in love?" She asks.

"Pfft," James chokes on the drink in his mouth, trying to suppress his laughter.

I glare at him until he starts to apologize.

"You really are in love," she says.

"No, I'm not; I'm just being a good friend," I defend myself, but that was clearly a wrong move.

"You didn't have to defend yourself," she laughs, "I can't believe it. Kevin is in love."

"If you have nothing else to do for me, could you leave," I say to her.

"Come on, his cheeks are red," she points out to James.

"I think he's furious now," James doesn't hesitate to join in.

"You two are annoying," I get up, ready to leave.

"Where are you going?" She asks.

"My job in New York is done," I answer, then turn to James, "You can handle everything while I'm gone, right?"

"Sure thing, boss," he replies.

As I leave, Sandra holds my arm, temporarily halting my movement.

"Are you happy with her?" She asks.

"It's not like that," I answer.

"Just assume it's like that," she says.

"Then yes, I am. She makes me happy," I reply with no hesitation.

"Then, I wish you the best of luck," Sandra says warmly.

Back in Malibu.

On my way to my place on the hills, I stop by a toy store to pick up some things for Alex. He likes whatever anyone gives him, but I'm considering getting him a bike.

"Would it be okay to give the son of a single mother a bicycle as a gift without her thinking you have any intentions for her?" I ask the salesperson.

"I wouldn't know that, sir," she answers.

"Can a four-year-old ride bikes?" I continue my questioning.

She visibly holds back the urge to laugh, "Yes. Many four-year-olds lean to ride a bike. I would recommend training wheels along with a bike so you can teach him how to ride it."

"I don't know how to ride a bike," I admit.

"I can give you a discount for two bikes." She offers.

It's about time I learn how to ride a bike, so I accept the offer.

Afterward, I visit a jewelry store. I need a new watch.

I'm sure she won't mind me getting her a gift.

Earrings, a necklace, and a watch. I can't decide what to get, so I buy all three.

"Is it for your wife?" The attendant asks as he gets me my receipt.

"No, she's a friend," I reply.

"Is that so?" He arches his brow, a smile tugging at the side of his face.

I ignore it and take the purchased items.

For my next stop, I'm torn between going straight home or maybe visiting her first to announce my return.

It would make more sense if I went to her place first. I know I'm not supposed to expect anything after what happened in New York, but a part of me hopes for something.

Years ago, I thought that I wouldn't want a relationship where I would have to settle down.

But now, being in a relationship and settling down sounds good to me.

Everyone was right; I have changed a lot.

I stop at her house, feeling more nervous about knocking on the door than when I asked a girl out for the first time in high school.

I ring the doorbell and wait.

"Coming!" I hear Alex's cheerful voice coming towards the door.

"Alex, I told you not to open the door," Lydia says, "just hold on, I'll get it."

As I open the door, I see her beautiful face again. Although it's been four days since I last saw her, it felt like I hadn't seen her face in years.

There's something different about her. The look in her eyes... they're the same as the first time we reunited.

"Is everything all right?" I ask, my tone laced with worry.

"You're back," she says, giving me a cold response.

I need some clarification. I am very confused...

ARROGANT BILLIONAIRE'S DO-OVER

Is this the same person I slept with in New York? I thought we'd finally started to share our feelings for each other.

"Yes, I'm back," I answer, trying to seem unfazed, "I brought some gifts for Alex."

Giving her the things I bought for her could be a bad idea.

"Oh," the deadpan response annoys me.

"Uncle Kevin!" Alex notices me, and Lydia moves out of the way to let him get to me.

As soon as her son hugs me, she retreats into the house.

"Did you get me anything? Did you fly in an airplane? Did you have a safe trip?" Alex attacks me with questions.

"The answer to all those questions is yes," I reply, forcing my attention onto the boy, "Is everything all right with your mom?"

"Hmm?" Alex is staring at me with a blank expression.

"Never mind," I sigh, "Let's go see your new bike."

I show him the gift I got for him, and he's ecstatic. After putting on the training wheels, he gets on the bike and tries to ride it.

I have absolutely no idea what I need to do to teach him how to ride a bike, so I pull out my phone to research.

"Will you be needing lunch and dinner?" Lydia asks. She's wiping her hands with a kitchen towel, her eyes on her son, before turning her attention to me.

"Yes, I do," I respond, "Are you going to work today? If not, maybe we can all go to my place and spend a day together."

I continue with a little bit of humor, "You wouldn't happen to know how to ride a bicycle, would you?"

"Unfortunately, my sister will take care of Alex today," she says.

The way she says it makes me feel like I'm an inconvenience.

"Oh, that's fine. Maybe we can practice some other time?" I'm now begging for her permission, "I have nothing else to do in Malibu."

"I'll think about it," she says, "Alex, lunch is ready."

"But I want to play some more with Uncle Kevin," her son protests.

Turning to me, she says, "Five minutes. And then let him come back in the house. Once my sister gets here, I will leave for your place."

"Okay," my shoulders drop.

She doesn't say anything else and returns to the house. Something happened.

"Push me!" Alex demanded.

"All right, here we go," I hold onto his shoulders and slowly push him.

It's okay; everything is fine. I don't know what happened, but I may be overthinking it.

"Mommy has been acting weird," Alex says.

"Did something happen?" I ask.

"I don't know," he shakes his head, "but a man came, and after he left, mommy hugged me, but she seemed sad."

A man? Is that why she's avoiding me? Is it someone I know who knows about her? Was I spied on at the amusement park? Is it the media? Are they trying to get their hands on her for an exclusive scoop?

I shake off my thoughts and try adjusting the training wheels.

"You must be Uncle Kevin," a woman says.

I look up and notice a taller version of Lydia staring down at me.

"Auntie, Lily!" Alex gets down from the bike and hugs the woman. She must be the tall young sister that Lydia was talking about.

"How are you doing, sport?" She ruffles his hair, and he tries to take her hands off his head but fails miserably.

"You must be Lydia's younger sister," I say as I get to my feet, "I would have loved to offer you a handshake, but my hands are dirty."

"It's fine. A pleasure to see the uncle spoiling my nephew," she smiles.

"He got me a bike," Alex announces.

"That's so cool," she says with a smile.

"I'll be on my way," I say to her.

"All right then, take care and see you soon, hopefully," she says.

Could she know about the man?

There's no need to ask her. I excuse myself and make my way to the car. I'm about to drive off when I notice Lydia coming out to welcome her sister.

As she notices me staring at her, she looks away immediately.

It hurts.

Oh boy, I really have changed if things like this hurt me.

CHAPTER 17

Tell Me Why

Kevin

"So what would you like for lunch?" asks Lydia.

As promised, she's in my house, ready to prepare my lunch.

"What would you recommend?" I ask, trying to match her desire to be professional.

"Going through your groceries, I can make you Chicken sandwiches," she says, "I know you are particularly fond of my fried rice, so I can make that as well."

"I'm not that hungry, so sandwich first, and the fried rice can be for dinner," I reply.

"Understood, just give me thirty minutes," she says when she gets to work.

I join her in the kitchen to help prepare the meal like usual.

"You don't have to do that; I'll handle it myself," she says.

"Okay, what exactly happened to you?" I ask, unable to hide my anger.

"What are you talking about?" She asks, feigning ignorance.

"I'm talking about how you're treating me right now and how you were behaving when I stopped by your house earlier today," I respond, "Did I do something?"

"You didn't do anything; I can't have a client making their own food," she says as she tries to open the refrigerator.

"Bullshit," I frown and close the refrigerator door, "What happened to you, Lydia?"

"Nothing happened!" She raises her voice.

"Not with that voice. Something must have happened," I say.

"It's none of your business," she says, "move aside."

"Not until you tell me what's wrong with you."

"This is no time to be stubborn," she says.

"I could say the same thing to you," I insist.

"Kevin," she calls my name with a warning, "Mind Your Business!"

"You are my business," I say to her.

"This is useless," she lets go of the fridge door, "If you don't want to have lunch now, then I might as well go home."

"Do not take another step," I warn, and she freezes.

I turn her head slowly to face me.

"Or what?" She stares back at me.

"Why are you upset with me?" I ask, "If I didn't do anything, did someone say something that made you upset with me?"

"I don't know what you're talking about," she says softly, looking away.

I hold her shoulders and make her face me, "Do you hate me, Lydia?"

"Why would you even ask that?" She returns, trying to free herself from my grip.

"Answer me."

"I don't hate you," she says.

"Then why are you looking at me like that?" I ask.

She's been staring at me with eyes of anger and contempt. But it's confusing because even though she's staring at me, it feels like she is looking at someone else and not me.

"It's not you," she confirms my suspicion.

"Then who?" I ask.

She falls silent, looking at the floor, refusing to answer me.

"Why won't you tell me what happened?" I ask.

"It's nothing serious... I'm just... it's not you, really," she says, her gaze and voice softening, resting her head against my chest, "I'm sorry."

"I don't need you to apologize," I said softly, "I just need you to tell me what exactly happened."

"I can't..." she whispers.

"It's okay," I let go of her arms, and she embraces me.

I hug her in response as well, and relief washes over me.

At least her anger wasn't towards me. She was just having a hard time dealing with her anger.

As she embraces me, her fingers dig into my back while she inhales deeply.

"Did I make you mad?" She asks.

"Kind of. I was really confused, and you did have me worried, thinking I had offended you," I reply.

"I'm sorry."

"Don't apologize," I remind her, "I'll wait until you're ready to talk. But if you have any problems, just speak to me, and I will listen. I will always listen."

"You're so different from the person I used to know years ago," she says, "you hardly listened to me back then."

"That's because I was stupid," I admit.

"We can both agree on that," she says with a dry chuckle, "I honestly thought you would never change. Now look at you."

She raises her head to look at me, and I notice her eyes are teary.

Instinctively, I wipe away the tears on her face, and she holds my hand, nuzzling her face against it.

Ever since our reunion, she has appeared to me as strong and capable of handling anything and everything by herself. But as of this moment, she seems so helpless. Her breathing is relaxed, and her eyes are closed. She's vulnerable.

I swallow hard.

Her eyes open slowly, and she stares at me. The look of innocence is the first time I've noticed it.

Her thumb gently caresses the back of my hand as she stares at me, causing my heartbeat to increase ever so slightly.

I want her.

"I see it in your eyes. You still want me," she says with a soft smile.

"No, that's not it..."

"It's okay," she whispers as she reaches for my right hand and places it on her breast. I can feel her heartbeat rise slowly, "It's okay. I want you to have me."

She's bluffing... right?

We already talked about this back in New York. It was only going to be a one-time thing.

Yes, I want to kiss her.

Yes, I want to make love to her.

I want to remind her body what happened in New York that night.

I want to make her feel what it's like to have her body under my control.

I want her to make love to me again.

But if I kiss her now, I would be preying on her moment of weakness.

Noticing my hesitation, she kisses my neck, "It's okay, one more time, that's all."

The words leave her lips, letting go of the chains holding me back with my reasons and releasing the desires that have been suppressed.

Our lips crash together, each of us seeming a bit more eager than the other.

It's a clumsy kiss.

My teeth hit against hers, and she's opening her mouth to take in more kisses.

We're struggling to maintain balance, so I pick her up, and she wraps her legs around my waist. While I'm carrying her to the living room, she's holding my face in her hand and kissing me furiously.

I settle her on the couch, and she stubbornly refuses to stop kissing me. It's okay, and I don't want her to stop kissing me, either.

She pauses the kiss, "inside me." She starts to pull down her pants, which I assist in helping her out of. As I take off my clothes, she takes off the rest of her clothes, then lays down on her belly, facing her ass towards me.

I touch her smooth yet soft ass, spreading her cheeks open slightly. The pink flesh makes a soothing, squishy sound as it opens.

She's already wet and doesn't need any further preparation.

I slid my dick into her, and she let out a moan.

"Just so you know," I say as I continue my insertion gently, "There's no one else around in this house. You can let out every sound until you feel better."

She doesn't say anything in response, but her pussy tightens with anticipation.

"Good girl," I praise with a growl as I sink my teeth into her neck.

"Mmm..." she moans, gently biting her teeth into the throw pillow.

I start to move. Her tightened insides resist and slow my movement, but I proceed anyway, and she slowly relaxes.

My thighs slapping against her ass fills the living room. She slowly raises her hips, turning her head to look at me; it seems like she wants to cry from the pleasure.

Her mouth slowly opens, her eyes pleading, and her voice stuck in her throat.

"Fuck," I frown and pull on her hair, making her look ahead, "Is this what you want? Then don't look at me like you want me to stop."

"I'm sorry...." She apologizes. Her hips move backward to reduce my pace, but I hold her in place, moving faster.

"You made me worried. For a moment, I thought you wanted me to stop," I continued my movements.

"Aww..., It's getting too much," she tries to push me away, but there's no point, "It's enough... I'm going to come too soon..."

"Oh, are you?" I grin as I pause my movement, then switch to alternating paces. Deep thrusts, shallow, faster, then slow, shallow. The inability to predict my thrusts makes her lift her upper body. I pull out and get seated.

"You..." she starts to say, holding onto my dick and slowly stroking it, "Shouldn't stop."

"I thought you said you had enough?" I smirk.

"I was lying," she says, "Do it again... Please..."

"No.... I've had enough," I reply, "If you want it, you have to do it yourself."

"Fine..." she says and positions herself to ride on my dick.

She leans back, using my legs as support, thrusting her hips.

Her eyes hold a seductive grin, while mine remains passive.

She starts to tighten her walls, a smirk on her face as she does so.

The sensation almost breaks my facial expression, but I keep it under control by closing my eyes. She starts moving faster. The innocent look is far gone from her eyes.

"Come on..." she teases, 'What happened to let my voice out until I'm satisfied?"

"Shut up," I frown and get to my feet. I flip her on her back, and her legs are now wrapped around my waist. It goes deep into her, hitting her insides at the perfect spots.

"Ah...ahh.. easy..." she pleads as her moans get louder.

But I don't relent, pinning her back against the couch. I continue to pound her. The juice from her sweet spot is overflowing, and her moans are getting louder and louder.

"Kisses... I want kisses..." she demands as I continue to move. I accept her request, kissing her deeply.

They seem different from the kisses from the other night. Or is it just me? I'm about to release, but I can't pull out now. I'll make it. Just a little more.

"You're perfect," she says, "Oh my god, it's so good."

Her words of praise catch me off guard, and I pull out, but it may have been too late.

"You don't have to worry," she says, "Let's keep going."

Usually, this is the part where one of us is supposed to do the reasonable thing and stop.

But if she won't do it, I won't either.

CHAPTER 18

The Unwanted Visitor

Lydia

He's asleep. Considering how long we went at it, I'm not surprised that he is asleep.

Staring at Kevin's sleeping face puts me to rest. I didn't expect that we would be having sex again so soon. I was going to stop, but seeing how much he was trying to hold back, I gave in to my desires.

The result is as expected. I feel a lot better. Being cold towards him was definitely not a good idea. He wasn't the reason I was upset.

Even now, when I think about what happened the other evening, I can slowly feel my anger creeping back.

Four Days Ago

Pepper spray in my hand, I opened the door, and there he was, holding a bouquet of roses in one hand and wearing a nervous smile.

I raised the pepper spray to his face and got ready to spray him if he steps any closer.

"Easy, it's not that bad, is it?" He asked as he raised both hands in defense.

"What the hell are you doing here?" I asked, "And your answer better be good."

"I just came to talk," he said, "I even brought you some flowers to show I mean no harm."

I looked at the flowers and back at his face. I wasn't buying it.

"I'm serious; please just listen to me," He pleaded.

I lowered the pepper spray, but I still kept my guard up.

"Thank you," he said, "how are you doing?"

"What do you want?" I urged him to get to the point.

"I really just came here to talk. Can I come in?" He asked.

"No, you're lucky that I opened the door, and I'm letting you stand there," I said.

"Mommy, I'm hungry," Alex complained as he made his way towards me. He paused, looked at the man, and then turned back to me, "Can I have some chocolate?"

"I'll make dinner. Just wait for me inside, sweetie," I replied.

He sighed and turned around.

"Aren't you going to introduce me to him?" The man shamelessly asked.

"And why in the world would I do that?" I asked.

"Because I'm his father," you answered with so much confidence that it actually disgusts me.

"Todd, what you are to him is non-existent," I said, "You've been absent from the moment I told you I was pregnant until today. Why choose now to identify you as his father?"

The man who has shown himself was none other than Todd.

He was the man I fell in love with after I left Kevin. Compared to Kevin, he was sweeter, kinder, and a lot more gentle. He seemed interested in my dreams and even helped me with my career by finding a culinary school and telling me where to get a job.

He filled me with so much hope that I thought that I had finally found someone to settle down with.

We even talked about our future together, and although he never proposed to me formally, he told me when he planned to marry me. It was better than Kevin, who never mentioned any plans at all.

And yet, when Todd found out I was pregnant, he told me we were too young to have kids. He pretended he was worried about my career and how the pregnancy might affect it, but the truth was he wanted nothing to do with the baby.

I expected his words to be somewhere along the lines of, "No matter what happens, I will be by your side."

But instead, he just disappeared without any contact information. His cell phone was turned off, and since I didn't know any of his friends or family, I couldn't contact them, either.

I was enraged.

And now, he is standing at the front door...

"Come to think of it, how did you even find my house?" I asked.

"I asked someone at your office," he answered.

"It couldn't have been Allison," I said.

"Who is that?"

"None of your concern," I glared, "if you have nothing else to do here, could you please leave?"

"Lydia, I've changed. You have to give me another chance," he demanded, "I was foolish five years ago, but now I want to take responsibility for you and our son. Don't take me out of his life."

"Why do you make it like I was the one who took you out of his life?" I asked, "Was I the one who told you to leave? Was I the one who suggested we were too young to have kids?"

"Look, that's in the past, and I'm sorry I behaved that way in the past," he said, "but you have to understand neither of us was ready to start a family."

"Neither of us?" I raised a brow. "Why are you including me in your own irresponsibility?"

"Come on, you were barely twenty-three," he rolled his eyes, "And I was only twenty-four. What did you think I was going to do? Jump in agreement."

"What did my age have to do with anything?"" I tried my best to keep my voice low, not to worry Alex, "I made it work at that age, didn't I? And now you think you can just walk back in here and be a father? I raised my son alone all these years."

"Then allow me to work for it," he placed his hand on my cheek, but I swatted it away and raised the pepper spray, "Have you forgotten the plans we made together? We were going to have a beach wedding."

"You selfish little prick. I wanted a normal church wedding. You're the one who wanted the beach," I frowned, "just get out."

"No, please...," he begged with a sad look in his eyes, "at least let me see Alex."

"No, I am never letting anyone who's hurt me in the past come back into my life again," I responded, "now get off my property, or I will call the cops."

"But..."

I slammed the door. My hands were shaking. I wanted to scream and yell.

"Mommy, what happened?" Alex asked.

"It's nothing," I replied shakily and embraced him.

Afterward, the words I said to Todd bothered me.

I told Todd that I would never let anyone who had hurt me in the past come back into my life again, but Kevin was the first one to hurt me in the past.

I started to doubt my decision to let Kevin in my life again and pushed him away, but Kevin found his way to open my heart again.

A week later, I am still waiting to hear from Todd.

Work has been going well. Allison and I are working together as the rest of our staff have alienated us.

"I'm getting sick of this," Allison finally admits as she eyes the rest of the staff.

This is the part where I usually chime in, but I don't feel so good.

I've been feeling dizzy and exhausted. I've also been fighting the urge to throw up.

My period should start this week, and I could have sworn that I had cramps last week.

"Waiting for your snarky remark," Allison says, "Is everything all right? You don't look so good."

"Everything is..." I stop talking and cover my mouth.

The nausea hits even harder.

ARROGANT BILLIONAIRE'S DO-OVER

I escape from the kitchen and race to the bathroom, heaving my guts into the toilet.

Oh no... no, no, no, no, no!

The feeling of dread hits as I throw up again.

"Jesus, Lydia, what did you eat?" Allison asked as she followed after me. She helps hold back my hair and gently rubs my back to aid the process.

"It's not the food..."

My boss allows me to leave early, so I head straight to the pharmacy on my way back. With shaky hands, I purchase a pregnancy test strip.

The girl behind the counter noticed my distress, "Oh dear," she says, "just stay calm. It's not the end of the world."

"Don't you think I know that?" I snap. I realize the harshness of my words, "I'm sorry if I sounded rude... I'm sorry."

"Trust me, that's not the worst I've heard from a customer," she laughs, "Just take it easy, okay."

"Okay," I force a smile and take the kit.

I return home, and luckily for me, Lily and Alex aren't home.

Alex is at Kevin's, and Lily has a date.

I rush to the bathroom to get tested. I already have an idea of what the results will be. After waiting a few minutes, the two bright red lines confirm my suspicion.

Just then, I'm faced with a new level of worry. I don't want this baby, but the timing is problematic.

What will Kevin say? Is he ready for this? What if he disappears as Todd did?

Chapter 19

What I Want

Kevin

"I wish I could go to the fun park again," Alex says.

"You want to go to an amusement park? Like the one in New York?" I ask.

"Mm-hmm," he nods approvingly, "can we go?"

"I'd love to, but it's past 4 p.m., and I don't think your mom would want us to go to New York tonight," I explain.

"Aww..." his shoulders drop.

He continues coloring something: a tiny square cardboard paper he asked me to cut.

Ever since I did that for him, he's moved to a corner of the living room and has been painting it, refusing to let me see his masterpiece.

Usually, I would just wait for him to finish, but this is the first time he's been this secretive, so my curiosity is piqued.

Also, I feel bored as he isn't playing with me. We've already ridden the bicycle this afternoon. While Alex can ride his bike effortlessly without the training wheels, I've yet to master balancing myself on a bike.

I can't let the four-year-old outdo me, can I?

Still, Lydia is late. She usually comes around eleven-thirty to prepare lunch and four to prepare dinner.

She's yet to arrive for lunch, but luckily, I had some leftovers that I can heat up.

I should call and make sure everything is okay. It's been six weeks since we made love on the couch, but we haven't completely returned to the relationship we used to have.

She's not cold to me anymore, though.

As I pick up my phone to dial her number, I can hear her car pull up in the driveway. She walks into the living room, and her eyes settle on Alex and me.

She looks worried about something.

"Good evening, Kevin," she extends a warm greeting.

I'm overthinking, as usual.

"Good evening, Lydia," I greet.

"Mommy! Good evening!" Alex greeted her with a hug.

I quickly glance over at the masterpiece that he's spent time drawing.

"Mommy, can we go to the amusement park we went to last time?" Alex asks.

"It's in New York," she says.

"I know, but..." he turns to look at me, then turns his attention back to his mother, motioning for her to lower her head.

She does as Alex instructs, and he whispers something to her.

I notice she keeps glancing at me as he explains his plans.

"Are you sure?" She asks, "Him?"

Alex nods repeatedly with visible excitement.

"We still can't go to New York," she sighs.

"But... he has a plane," Alex whines, "And I really, really want to."

"What exactly did he say to you?" I ask.

"No telling?" Alex asks Lydia.

"I'm not going to tell," she promises.

"I don't like being left out of the plans, especially if they have something to do with me," I tell them. My phone pings, drawing my attention while Lydia and Alex try to reach some kind of agreement.

"We can't go tonight and return on the same day," she tries to explain, "He might be wealthy, but it's still a lot of money."

Checking the notification, James sent me a flyer; there's a special magic show here in Malibu—the same performer from New York.

"I guess it's a no, then," Alex's shoulders drop in disappointment.

"I wouldn't be so sure, buddy," I inform Alex.

"You want us to go to New York?" Lydia raises a brow in question.

"No, right here in Malibu," I respond and show her the flyer, "Your magical friends from New York are in the city. Who knows? Maybe they'll show you real magic tonight?"

"I knew there was no such thing as magic!" She insists as her face turns red from embarrassment again.

"Whatever you say, Miss Abracadabra," I shrug, and she gives me a pouting look.

"Can we go?" Alex asks, oblivious to his mother's embarrassed expression.

"Fine, we can," she gives in.

"All right," I get to my feet, "Do you two need to go home and change?"

"I'm okay," she replies, "Alex, where's your jacket?"

"In the dining room," he answers and races to get it.

I'm alone with Lydia. There's something odd. It feels like she has something on her mind.

"Want to talk about it?" I ask.

"What?" She blinks twice, "Oh, no. Don't mind me. It's been a rough day at work."

"Has everyone been treating you okay?" I ask.

"Very okay," she assured me, "I'm just a little tired."

"We can reschedule," I advise, "Maybe I shouldn't have suggested the magic show."

"No, the magic show is perfect," she says, "Don't worry about me."

"You're doing it again, pushing me away," I tell her, "Remember, I told you I'd always be here to listen."

"You did promise," she affirms, "But this isn't something I can tell you about that easily. It's not that I don't trust you or I won't respect your suggestion. I'm just concerned what your reaction will be."

"I understand," I say, but in reality, I don't understand.

"You don't have to pretend to understand," she chuckles softly, seeing through my facade, "But thank you."

"You're welcome," I smile, "I'll go get my things."

I make my way upstairs to my bedroom. After changing into my desired outfit, I paused and reflected on what Lydia just said.

Basically, she had something to tell me, and it's related to me. But she's worried that my response to what she has to say would be negative.

Now that I think about it, I'm facing the same issue Lydia is facing.

"I still haven't given her what I brought for her," I say to myself, noticing the gifts I bought for her, but I haven't been able to give them to her since I'm not certain what her reaction will be.

The magic show had a much bigger crowd than expected. Luckily, we could get there on time and secure the front-row seats.

This show started, and the magicians gave their hearts out in their performances.

I expected Lydia to be indifferent towards the performance, but she worked every part of it with childlike excitement.

I don't really get magic shows, but watching Alex and Lydia have fun was enough for me.

The magic show also featured an animal petting zoo. So patrons could play with some of the magical animals.

"Look at this uni-bunny!" Lydia smiles, trying to hold the bunny wearing a unicorn horn.

"That is clearly a bunny," I point out.

"No, it's an uni-bunny," she insisted.

"And this uni-puppy," Alex showed me the toy poodle wearing a unicorn horn, "can we have this puppy?"

"Are they for sale?" I ask the clerk.

"No sir, they are not," he replies.

"Sorry, Alex," I apologize, "maybe I'll get you a puppy and buy it a unicorn horn."

"Yay!" He jumps in excitement.

"You spoil him too much," Lydia pinched my elbow.

"Ow! Is that a bad thing? He's a good boy most of the time," I state.

Alex puts down the puppy and goes to his mother's side, "Mommy, where is it?"

"Now is not a good time," she says, "on our way home, you can have it."

"What exactly are you two up to?" I ask.

"It's a secret," they chorus in response.

"By the way, you're not getting a puppy," Lydia says, "you have to do the house plant test first."

"What's that?" Alex asks.

"Do people really do that?" I scoff.

"It's an essential test to check if you're ready to handle pets. You need to make sure you can take care of our house plants for a year without killing them. You need to give them the right amount of water every week, okay? " Lydia explains to Alex, ignoring me.

"I'll do it," Alex agrees.

"That's my boy," Lydia praises, "Now let's get something to eat."

Alex returns to me and stretches out his arms towards me, and I lift him up, allowing him to sit on my shoulder as we explore the rest of the show's attractions.

It's over.

We retreated to my house as most of their things were left there.

Alex is tired and will need to sleep soon.

"I forgot…" he says to his mum.

"Oh, here you are," she hands him a card, "So sorry."

He thanks her and brings the card to me, "It's for you, Uncle Kevin."

I recognize the cardboard as the same one he's been working on today.

The card is folded neatly, and I open it up.

It reads;

"Happy Father's Day, Uncle Kevin.

Thank you for the toys.

Thank you for the fun.

Thank you for the big plane.

Thank you for coming to my daycare for the Father's Day event.

I love you."

The roof is leaking because my face suddenly feels wet. Or am I sweating?

"Don't tell me you're crying," Lydia laughs.

"I'm not. Don't be ridiculous," I say to her with a frown, but it has no effect as she's already seen through me.

"Do you like it?" Alex asks while he rubs his eyes.

"I love it. Thank you, and I love you, too," I answer.

He yawns and hugs my leg. I pick him up and settle him in my arms, where he drifts to sleep.

"You've never received a letter before?" Lydia continues her teasing.

"Not like this, I haven't," I answer honestly.

Even when my father was alive, I don't recall giving him a letter like this. There is so much sincerity that it melts my heart.

I make a mental note to have the letter framed and hung up in my office in New York.

"Can you two sleep over tonight?" I request.

"Sure," she agrees.

After tucking Alex into bed, I watch the little boy fall asleep. He really made my day today.

I feel bad for missing out on something like this when she presented the opportunity to be in a committed relationship and start a family years ago.

I've no one to blame but myself.

All I can do now is wait and hope that we can have a future where I can watch Alex sleep and wake up to Lydia by my side, and maybe we can have more children together.

Lydia kisses me on the cheek, taking me by surprise.

"What was that for?" I ask, "Although I'm not complaining."

"Of course you wouldn't complain," she sighs, "just take it as a thank you for making his day again."

"You know something like this won't be bad," I admit, "part of me regrets turning down the offer to start a family a long time ago."

"What did you just say?" She asks.

"I was just thinking out loud," I defend myself.

She holds my chin, makes me face her, and then kisses me again.

She pulls back and stares at me while smiling.

I lean in for the second kiss.

CHAPTER 20

Another Man

Kevin

Something is definitely wrong.

Lydia suddenly stopped coming in the mornings. She took permission, but for someone as diligent as her, it's still a strange thing.

"And that's why you called me?" James asks.

"You're the relationship expert, so tell me what I'm supposed to do," I instruct him.

"What happened to the magic words of please and thank you?" He asks, feeling a little cocky.

'Don't test my patience with me' is what I want to say, but I swallow my pride and instead say, "Please, can you tell me what to do?"

"Absolutely no idea what is wrong with her," he says.

"You useless little...." I pause and deeply breathe, "You could have just started with that."

"Don't look at me. I have never dated any of my staff or chef," he says matter-of-factly, "but if you're asking me for advice, then it must be really bad."

"I know I was telling myself the same thing," I say with an exasperated sigh, "I didn't know I would be this concerned about a woman."

"Isn't life a bitch," he adds.

"I know, and I'm not laughing," I tell him.

"Do you think it's something you did?"

"The first time she said it wasn't me, but the second time, I don't know," I reply.

"Maybe you forgot something important about her life," he adds, "You mentioned the tools you used to use to date sometime in the past, right?"

"Right."

"So maybe there's something important to her that she's expecting you to remember, but you didn't," he explains, "a birthday perhaps?"

"Lydia is not that petty to be cold because I forgot about a birthday," I reply.

"But it may bother her if you were her romantic interest," he explains, "Oh!"

"What? What did you figure out?" I ask.

"Maybe while you were in New York, she found someone she was interested in?" He replies.

"You must be out of your mind," I frown.

"Relax, sir," he tries calming me down, "Think about it for a second. Nothing really changed from your end. You've always been busy with your business. She's had a baby with another man, and maybe she was still in love with him. But after working with you for some time, her feelings for you started to come back. And while you were in New York, this guy returned to her life, and she realized that maybe she loves him more than you."

It's just a theory, but hearing about it makes me think it's possible for a second.

"No, that's not possible. If that was the case, she wouldn't have slept with me when I got back," I tell James.

"Sir, it's only a theory," he insists, "if you're not sure of what's going on, you'll need to ask Ms. Lydia herself to clear your doubts."

"You're right. You're right," I nod, a feeble attempt to dispel the negative thoughts.

As the phone call ends, I cannot stop thinking that Lydia has someone else in her life.

"And that's all for lunch. Sorry, I missed breakfast again," Lydia apologizes.

"Is everything okay?" I ask.

She looks exhausted and, in a way, looks sick. I can tell that there's something important she's still hiding.

"I'm okay," she says, "you worry too much."

"I think I'm allowed to worry," I say softly.

"And I'm glad that you do." She says with a soft smile, "Please watch over Alex for me this afternoon."

"Yes, ma'am," I salute.

"Thanks," she squeezes my cheek before leaving.

With an exhausted sigh, I take a seat on the sofa.

"Mommy is still sad?" Alex asks.

"Is she like that at home as well?" I ask.

"Sometimes she sits down and stares at nothing," he replies, "but she says everything is okay."

"Yeah, I kind of got that feeling," I sigh. *Is Lydia really going to make both of us worry?*

"Maybe it's because her birthday is coming up," he says.

I recall James saying something similar.

"Does she look forward to her birthday?" I ask.

"All the time," he beams with a smile, "I always make her birthday cards. But this time, I want to get her a gift, too."

It might be an excellent opportunity to give her the gifts I bought for her.

"Do you know the gift you want to get for her?" I ask him.

"I do. But Uncle Kevin, don't you want to give her anything?" He asks.

"I don't know what your mom would like, so we could go together and buy her a gift. What do you say?" I ask.

"Sounds good to me!"

I still have no idea what's bothering her. If it is her birthday that is getting her depressed, then maybe I'm not the only one who has changed.

Alex's idea of a perfect birthday gift for his mom is a spatula. It's a perfect gift for someone who loves cooking. For a four-year-old, it's pretty impressive.

I found some oven mitts with the initials 'R' on them. And with that, we're done with the birthday gift shopping.

"Let's get some crayons and paper to make her birthday cards," I suggest.

"Okay, I know where the art shop is," he says, grabbing my hand and leading me in the right direction.

"Is that Alex?" A man asks.

He looks like he's in his late 20s or early 30s and has light brown hair, blue eyes, and a lean build. For some reason, I don't get a good vibe from him. There's something sinister and off-putting about it.

Cautiously, I pull Alex to my side.

"Why are you with him?" The stranger asks with an annoyed look on his face.

"Do you know him?" I ask Alex.

"It's one of those situations where I know him, but he doesn't know me," the man replies, as he lowers and extends his hand towards Alex, but Alex pulls away and hides behind my leg.

"Oh, dear." The man sighs, looking annoyed.

"Could you step away, please?" I asked politely. I am ready to call the police if he doesn't obey.

"You should be the one stepping away," he says as he returns to his feet, "Old man."

"I don't think my age has anything to do with this," I say, realizing he's not worth the trouble, "Let's go, Alex."

I don't let Alex walk anymore. Instead, I lift him into my arms. Alex hugs me while cautiously keeping his eyes on the stranger.

"Say hello to Lydia for me," the man says, "tell her Todd sends his regards."

I do not have the time to interrogate him on how he knows her, so I ignore him and continue moving.

As we put ourselves a reasonable distance away, Alex finally relaxes.

"That was the guy who came to the house," he tells me, "Mommy has been acting weird since then."

"I see."

I can only hope that James wasn't right.

As Lydia returns to make dinner, I decide to tell her what happened.

"Oh God, Todd met you guys?" She asks with anger in her eyes.

"Who is he?" I ask, "He didn't meet with us. He just ran into us."

"He is no one," she says dismissively.

"That doesn't seem to be the case," I point out, "Alex also mentioned that he had been at your house after our trip to New York. And ever since he visited, you've been sad and angry."

"You have to tell me if something is wrong," I continue, "If you need help, please let me know, and I will help."

"And I'm saying I don't need your help," she insists, "there isn't anything for you to worry about. I can handle this, please."

"It's a lot to take in, I know, but I'm fine," she continues.

"There's no getting through to you, is there?" I'm exhausted, "fine, I'll let you handle it."

"And I will handle it," she says, making it sound like I was doubting her ability to do so.

I don't know who Todd is, but I don't plan on sitting back and letting anyone ruin our chances of being happy.

Chapter 21

Do You Want Me To Stay?

Lydia

"You're pregnant?!" Lily raises her voice.

"Shhh!" I cover her mouth and look around us.

We're at my home, and Alex is fast asleep.

"How could this have happened?" She asks as she swats my hand away from her mouth.

"Oh, Lily," I start to say, "you see when a man and woman love each other so much..."

"Don't joke around. You know what I mean. This is serious," she frowns, "this is the second time you became pregnant without being married. I swear to God. If it's Todd again... How could you let him change your mind so quickly? He just showed up out of the blue, and you're already pregnant with his baby? You said you would never let him come back in your life again."

"Oh hush," I shush her, "do you think your older sister is that dumb?"

"No."

"Then have faith in me," I say with a shrug, "of course it's not Todd."

"Kevin?" She asks.

I nod.

"Okay. Then there is no problem, right?" Lily shrugs.

"Wait, why is it not a problem?" I ask.

"Aren't you in love with him?" she gives me a questioning look.

"Who says I am?"

"I don't have enough energy to argue with you on this," she sighs, "have you told Kevin?"

"I can't." I sigh.

"Why not? He deserves to know," she says, "and how far pregnant are you?"

"About six weeks. I just found out."

She stares at me like I've lost my mind, "You know you're pregnant with the guy you really care about, and you still haven't told him?"

"Because I'm scared that what happened to me with Todd will happen again," I respond, "Kevin is nice to me now, but being responsible for a baby is totally different. He might just leave me once he finds out I'm pregnant."

"I don't think he would do that." Lily insists.

"Last time I checked, you aren't Kevin, and I'm not in love with him," I insist.

"Sis, I know you," she says softly, "you are not the kind of girl who will sleep with anyone without any relationship. And I know how much you started hating going to Peak Bites, but you seem still happy being Kevin's personal chef. You enjoy leaving Alex with him, and every time Alex talks about Kevin, you are excited."

Lily tells me all the valid facts, but I refuse to say anything.

"Also, did you hear the news?" she asks.

"What news?"

"He gave the Sandra actress a role in his new project," she informs me, "which means the scandal issue is over. He has no other reason to remain in Malibu."

I've been hoping that it will take a long time to resolve the scandal issue and fooling myself into thinking that Kevin will always be here.

I was not in a hurry to tell Kevin about my pregnancy, but now this has changed everything. Knowing he's about to leave puts me in a state of panic.

"I can see it in your eyes now. You don't want him to go, do you?" She asks.

"I need to go get some air," I end the conversation, excusing myself.

"That's what I thought...," she sighs.

Grabbing my car keys, I enter the road.

At first, I drove in circles to get my mind in order.

Is telling Kevin about the pregnancy still a good idea? If I remember correctly, he mentioned regretting losing the chance to have a family with me. Is that his way of saying he wants to try again?

After a few minutes of driving, I find myself in front of his house.

"I am so not ready for this," I sigh and get out of the car, making my way to his front door.

I press the doorbell.

After a few seconds of waiting, he opens the door. He's shirtless, and the beads of sweat on his body cause him to glimmer.

"Hey," he's out of breath.

"Hey," I reply, "are you busy?"

"No, not really," he answers as he steps away, letting me into the house.

As I entered the house, I noticed the moving boxes.

Is he leaving?

"I hear the case with Sandra has been settled," I start the topic.

"Yeah, it has, so that means I can return to New York," he replies, "Malibu has been fun."

"So, are you going to leave?" I ask.

"Well, I guess..." he replies.

My shoulder sinks, and my face dims with sadness.

"Is everything okay?" He asks.

"Yes, everything is fine," I pout as I look away.

"Do you want me to stay?" He asks as he holds my chin, making me face him, "Is someone missing me already?"

"So full of yourself," I move his hand away from my chin, but he wraps his arms around my waist and pulls me to him.

"Why are you here, Lydia?" He asks.

"You're sweaty. Get away from me," I place my hand on his chest and try to move him away, but I can't take my hand off.

"I need to know why you're here," a cocky smile on his face annoys me.

"I didn't come to visit you. I was just in the neighborhood," I lie.

"This house is on my private land. There is no neighborhood," he reminds me, "you can just admit that you wanted to see me. Or maybe you don't want me to leave? Is my little Lydia missing me that much?"

"I'm not little," I protest.

"Is that so?" He kisses my forehead, sending me shock waves, "Sorry about that. You're just too irresistible."

I frown at him. It's a useless frown and one that does not affect him whatsoever.

"Do you want me to stay?" He asks.

I don't want to answer. I want him to stay, but I don't want to be seen as desperate.

"That's a no then," he sighs.

I start feeling a bit dizzy as I see him picking up one of the boxes.

If he leaves now, I'll have to deal with being at that restaurant with people who hate me. Alex is going to miss him terribly. And I won't have anyone who makes me feel so at peace. And I won't have someone who'd be ready to kiss me whenever I'm vulnerable. And if he leaves now, how am I going to tell him about this baby?

I grab his arm, and he stops to turn and look at me.

The look in his eyes says he's won.

But I don't care.

"Don't make me say it," I whisper.

"You don't have to say it," he says.

I take a good look at the exposed chest. His sweat has begun to dry off.

I kiss his collarbone and even bite down hard on it.

"Ouch, that hurts, you know?" He complains as he whimpers in pain.

I leave his collarbone alone and go for his chest, sucking on his nipples.

He strokes my hair gently while I work on his nipples. Judging by how he's flinching so much from getting sucked, his nipples are very sensitive. And now, mine have started to demand attention as well.

I lower myself to my knees and pull down his sweatpants and reveal his dick. I take off my shirt, then tackle him down to the floor.

Kevin starts to suck my breasts slowly. They have gotten slightly bigger and tender from the pregnancy, and I let out a moan. He starts to play with my nipple with his tongue while teasing my other nipple with his fingers.

I grab his pulsating dick in my hand and beg him to come inside, but he is not done pleasing me first.

His kisses move down to my belly and to my navel until he reaches my panties. He opens my leg and stares at my wet pussy through my panties first. Then, with one swift motion, he takes my panties off. I let out a loud moan as he buries his face between my legs, and in response, I grab his head and push him down into my pussy deeper.

I arch my back every time his tongue does its magic on my pussy, and my moans are getting louder and louder. I scream when he finds my clit and starts sucking it intensely.

I feel like I'm on a different level of high right now. My eyes are in a confused state, my mouth open in lustrous wonder, and my moans don't stop getting louder.

I grab his head up towards my face and beg him, "Come inside, I can't hold much longer," as my hand grabs his throbbing dick again.

He grins and makes eye contact as he shoves his monstrous seven-inch all the way in one move.

"Uhhh...," I grab his buttocks and bring him closer. My nails are digging into his skin, and I can feel his muscles tightening and loosening as he pounds me repeatedly.

My body gives in to lust, and I start moving faster to make him move faster, but he pulls out and commands, "Ride me. Start slow."

I slowly sink myself into him, and I hear him moan. While making eye contact, I take time before I start moving fast again. I move my hips in a circular motion so he can feel every part of my inside.

"Aw..., fuck..." he's moaning tells me he is getting closer, but I know he can still take the faster movements.

"Were you always this big?" I ask while panting.

"Were you always this tight?" He retorts, gripping my waist to help himself get the upper hand.

He starts to control my movement, grinding me against him while stirring up my insides.

It feels so good my head starts to spin.

I don't want him to leave. I've become too attached to allow him to leave.

Who's going to hold me like this? Who will help me get out of a funk when I'm having a bad day? Who will spend time with me in the kitchen, making mistakes and learning from them as I instruct him? Who will look at me the way he does?

"I'm not going anywhere," he assures me as he reaches his climax, filling me up, and I join him in total ecstasy.

We kiss like it's the first time we've ever kissed.

"One more?" He asks.

"I'll have to catch my breath," I reply as I slowly get off him.

If I wasn't already pregnant, no amount of birth control was going to stop me from getting pregnant.

I collapse and lay next to him.

"What's with these boxes?" I ask.

"Oh, I was never planning to move back to New York," he replies, "These are some of my stuff from my house in New York. I was just sorting the arrived items until you arrived."

He... wasn't planning on leaving?

While I feel the urge to snap his neck in half, I'm happy that I don't have to worry about losing him.

Chapter 22

Do As I Say

Lydia

Finally, a sigh of relief. Realizing that Kevin isn't leaving has put me in a calm state.

I panicked and thought he was leaving, and I ended up sleeping with him, but it helped me get the plan Kevin had in mind.

His contract with me as his personal chef is coming to an end, so he tells me to notify my boss about extending my services. This will give me the chance to decline the mayor's offer so that my boss can service the mayor.

"So your client is extending his contract," my boss asks.

"Yes, and he's paying double as usual," I reply, "That's double the amount the mayor is offering to pay."

"You sure are in high demand. Many clients ask for you," he remarks.

"That's because the team advertises me well," I defend, "the rest is good luck, and I always do my best to satisfy my clients."

"So it seems," his emotionless response tells me he is not impressed with my excuse.

It doesn't matter just as long as I get to work outside of this building. As I leave his office, Allison meets up with me.

"Is it just me, or have you started working on thin ice in this restaurant?" She asks playfully, but I can sense the worry in her tone.

"I have absolutely no idea why any of them will be so upset with me," I sigh.

"It's more of a jealousy thing," she explains.

"And why are they jealous?" I frown, "When I get more clients than you, you don't get jealous of me. You sometimes get the clients I want, but I'm not jealous of you."

"That's because we both know the amount of hard work each other put in. I think the rest of them are just blind to the hard work we put in," she explains with a sigh, "as for the boss, you would think he would be grateful that we bring in many customers for him."

"And then there's a mayor who seems to make things worse with his request," I add.

"You really aren't getting any break, are you?" she sighs. "Speaking of which..." She pauses and leans closer. "How far along are you in your pregnancy?"

ARROGANT BILLIONAIRE'S DO-OVER

"What makes you ask?"

"You don't need to play dumb with me," she sighs, "In fact, I'm disappointed that you didn't come to me to share the news. I'm your best friend. I will always support you no matter what."

"It's fine. I just didn't want to bother anyone," I admit, "also I didn't..."

"You didn't want to tell me because of my fertility issues, correct?" She asks as if she was expecting me to say that. "I understand your fear, but you should know that you're my best friend. If you're happy, I'm happy. I'm always here for you."

"I'm really sorry," I admit, "please forgive me."

"It's already forgiven. But please tell me who the father is..., please," she pleaded, even faking tears.

"Remember that client who paid double for my services?" I ask.

"Oh my god! Kevin Wills? I was not expecting that at all," she remarks in honest surprise, "How can it be? I thought you didn't like him."

"I didn't..."

"But?" She wiggles her brows.

"But he's changed, okay?" I groan.

"Knowing you, you haven't told him you're pregnant with his baby," she rolls her eyes.

"I can't tell him. You know it's against company policies to date a client," I remind her. "also, I don't want to rush things. He's my ex-boyfriend from eight years ago, and I walked out on him, okay?"

"You dated Kevin Wills eight years ago, and you walked out on him?" she responds with her eyes wide open.

I don't say anything, but my grin confirms the statement.

"Shut up! Really?" She blinks twice, "And now you're carrying his baby?"

"Shhhh... Keep it down," I hush the over-excited friend.

"That's it. I know you're pulling my legs," she sighs, "thank you for entertaining me this evening."

"You're welcome."

It's nice to have someone I can talk to besides my sister. I always wanted to tell Allison, but as I mentioned, I was worried about reminding her of her infertility. Well, it turns out I was worried for nothing.

I'm back home.

Alex is sleeping over at Kevin's. They plan to have a boys' night out or something like that. I think he's letting me have some time for myself, hoping it will help me summon the courage to talk to him about what's been bothering me.

For someone who used to be so grumpy and selfish, he does know his way when it comes to being kind and understanding.

I make myself dinner at home, and I realize it's been a while, considering I've been having dinner at Kevin's almost every night.

I make a simple, easy salad for me and my baby. I look through the old cookbook containing recipes I created when I was pregnant with Alex. Each meal has enough nutrition for me and the baby.

Without Kevin to help me prepare the dinner, it's taking me a bit longer. It tells you how much I've become accustomed to having him around.

I miss preparing meals with Kevin...

The sound of the doorbell ruins the perfect evening.

As I open the door, it only gets worse.

"What are you doing here, Todd?" I ask as I see him standing outside.

"Why is it that a stranger like him can hold our son, and I can't?" He asks.

"What do you want, Todd?" I ignore his question and repeat mine.

"I want custody," he says it like it makes sense.

"You will get no such thing," I assure him.

"You can't just deny me of seeing our son," he says.

"I think I can," I smirk, "And really, stop calling him *our* son. He's mine and only mine ever since you walked out on us and lost contact four years ago. You didn't even want me to keep the baby, remember?"

He looks like he's about to lose his mind, and I really don't care.

I won't let Todd ruin my evening.

"There is something you don't know about," he says with a confident grin. "Don't you think it's odd how you were able to get a job at Peak Bites in the first place?"

"What are you talking about now?"

"Well, my uncle is your boss," he announces.

It's a bit strange, but I guess it makes sense, considering both of them want to make my life miserable.

"Where are you going with this?'" I ask.

"When I saw that playboy client of yours, I did some digging and found out that the two of you are together," he explains, "you aren't supposed to be sleeping with your clients now, are you?"

He's been spying on me and Kevin.

This spells more trouble for Kevin than for me because he has just finished resolving the scandal with Sandra, and he does not want another round of unfavorable media attention immediately after."

"What do you want?" I frown.

"There we go," he says with a satisfied look on his face, "like I've been trying to tell you, I want the custody of Alex, and I want us to get back together."

He might be bluffing about the whole thing, so there's no way to fully trust him.

"I think I'll take my chances," I say to him and close the door.

"Don't say I didn't warn you," his voice causes me to panic a little.

I had trouble sleeping last night. Todd's visit is still upsetting me.

As I arrive at the Peak Bites to report, the boss suddenly asks for me.

"Well, my uncle is your boss," I remember Todd's announcement.

I tried to act all tough last night, but now I think I might be in trouble.

"Lydia, I want you to convince your client to terminate his contract with you," my boss says with a cold, expressionless face.

Normally, I will try to say anything to defend myself, but I can't. I'm afraid it would complicate things even more.

"I'll see what I can do, sir," I say to him.

"Not you'll see what you can do. Just do it as I asked," he insists.

"I will."

Chapter 23

Sudden Change

Kevin

I didn't expect her to come to my house that night, and it was a pleasant surprise to hear that she wanted me to stay.

Maybe it's a sign that something has finally started blossoming between us. I can't deny that I have fallen in love with Lydia. Not a moment goes by without thinking about her.

Each time I go to bed, I wake up looking forward to seeing her again in my house. Sometimes,

I feel like Lydia is my wife making me delicious meals, and Alex is our son. The opportunity to extend the contract with her fills me with joy.

"Maybe Lydia and Alex can live with me," I say to myself.

ARROGANT BILLIONAIRE'S DO-OVER

I want to have her by my side when I go to bed and when I wake up. She makes me realize that maybe there is more to life than being a playboy. I don't know how to tell her these feelings, and a part of me believes that telling her my feelings will ruin what we have now.

And yeah, I need to put her career into consideration as well.

I'm lost in my thoughts when my phone starts to ring.

Seeing it's Lydia, I answer immediately.

"Good morning, sir," she greets.

It throws me off because she sounds so formal. It's been a while since she called me sir.

"Is everything all right, Lydia?" I ask, "Did you check the number? Is this call for me?"

I'm assuming she meant to call some other client but ended up calling my number by mistake.

"Yes, I checked the number, Mr. Wills," she replied.

"Huh? Are you okay?"

Maybe she's at the restaurant and trying to keep our conversations professional.

"Does this have to do with the extension of your services?" I ask.

"Yes," she answers, "I need you to cancel the extension."

"What? Cancel the extension? Why?"

"No particular reason. That's the instruction I received from my management. I'm sorry, sir." She says.

Something's definitely not right. "Where are you?" I ask.

"Home," she says. If she is at home talking to me like this, something's definitely wrong.

"Do you really want me to cancel?" I ask.

"Yes, I do. And could you please take care of it quickly?" Lydia responds.

"Just stay right there; I'll be over shortly," I say to her.

I hang up the phone and immediately leave for her house. It can't be the same person talking to me. The same person who panicked, thinking I was going to leave. The same person who was excited when I announced we were extending our contract.

There's no way she wants me to cancel the extension of the contract.

I need to hear her say it in person.

I arrive at her home. After ringing the bell for a while, she finally answers. The look on her face tells me she's been forced to act in a way she doesn't want to.

ARROGANT BILLIONAIRE'S DO-OVER

"What was that call all about?" I ask, "Do you really want me to end the contract?"

She swallows hard, "Yes, I would like you to end the contract extension."

"If the pay is the problem, I can triple it," I offer.

"The pay isn't the problem," she explains, "I just can't be around you anymore."

"Uncle Kevin!" Alex notices me and tries to make his way towards me, but she stops him.

"Go back to your room, sweetie. Uncle Kevin and I need to have a grown-up conversation," she tells him.

Alex is more confused than I am, but he obeys his mother anyway and returns to the house while occasionally glancing back at us.

"Lydia, you're doing it again," I remark, "You're pushing me away without telling me what's going on. How many times do I have to tell you that I'm here for you if you need me?"

"Sorry, I can't listen to what you have to say," she says.

"I can't believe you because...," I say to her, "your face looks like you're in so much pain when you ask me to cancel the contract."

"Just leave, please." She covers her face, "You need to allow me to handle this on my own."

"This is beyond what you can do by yourself," I state, "It involves me also. Just tell me exactly what's bothering you, and I will help."

"There is nothing you can help," she stubbornly insists, "and if you want to help me, you can go back to New York and continue with your playboy lifestyle."

"You don't mean that," I shake my head in disbelief.

"Yes. I. Do." Her spelled-out response finally gets the message across. I'm not needed.

"If that's what you mean then," I say softly and turn around, "can I say goodbye to Alex at least?"

"No," she says.

Her face looks like she's on the verge of tears.

I just want to help her, but she won't let me.

"I see," I sigh, "Goodbye, Lydia."

"Goodbye, Kevin."

After I heard what Lydia had to say in person, I returned to New York.

"Good evening, and welcome back to New York," James greets, "you mentioned that the next time you come back, you would be coming back with Ms. Lydia and Alex. What's going on?"

"That is what I want to know," I reply, "Lydia forced me to cancel the contract with her. Her company refunded the money, and I tried reaching out to them, but no one will tell me why Lydia requested the cancellation."

"Did you do something?" James asks.

"I honestly don't think so, but if I did something, I'd like to know," I say.

"Maybe she made a major mistake, and they want to have her replaced with another staff member," James offers a theory, "that kind of thing sometimes happens."

"If that's the case, why didn't they assign someone else? Why do they ask me to cancel the contract and refund the money? I was paying double. It makes no sense." I shrug.

"True," James pauses to think about it, "Did she say anything?"

"She just told me she didn't want to be around me anymore, and that was the end of the story," I sigh.

"I got it! Blackmail. She must have been blackmailed," he says.

"What?" I raise a brow, "why would someone blackmail her to get to me."

"No one is getting to you through her," he sighs, "I think someone might have found out about your relationship and threatened her with it."

"Who could it be?" I ask, "The only people who seem to know about our relationship are people who were at the daycare for the Father's Day presentation and her younger sister."

"It could be any one of them," he says, "Do you want me to hire a private investigator to get to the bottom of this?"

"It's none of them," I assure him.

"There has to be someone who is threatening Lydia," James insists, "think hard about it, sir. Did you miss anyone who might know about your relationship with Lydia?"

I pause to think about it, but I can't think of anyone else at the moment. Despite being somewhat of a celebrity, no one really noticed me while I was in Malibu. My house is in the middle of private land, and I have no neighbors.

I visited Lydia's house only a few times, and I didn't interact with anyone in her neighborhood.

Whoever threatens Lydia must have thought about her job and our relationship.

And then it hits me.

"Find me everything you can about a man named Todd," I instruct, "Light brown hair, blue eyes, lean build. He was upset to see me with Lydia, so I think he was her ex-boyfriend."

"We'll do our best, sir," he says and gets to work.

As he leaves me alone in my office, I take a deep breath and think about my next steps. I know I said I'd let her handle this alone, but it's also affecting me.

"Why didn't you let me talk to Alex at least?" I'm talking to myself. It still hurts me to think that she doesn't trust me enough to help her with the problem.

"Sir?" James peeks into the office, "Ms. Lydia did not push you away because you did something wrong or she didn't like you anymore. Maybe she was conscious of your recent scandal issue, and the blackmailer took advantage of it to threaten her. She still cares for you, and this is her way of protecting you."

Oh..., I didn't think about it like that.

"Thanks, James." I say to him, "You really are the best assistant. When we find out who is responsible for this, I will let you punch him first."

Like I said earlier, I know she wants to handle this on her own, but what kind of man allows the woman he loves to fight the battles alone?

Chapter 24

No More

Lydia

"Why didn't you let me see Uncle Kevin?" Alex asks as soon as Kevin leaves.

"It's very complicated, sweetie," I say to him, "You have to understand mom is doing this for your own good. And for Uncle Kevin, too."

"You don't want to see Uncle Kevin again?" My poor baby looks like he's about to cry.

"Please don't cry," I plead with him as I hug him.

"Do you hate him?" He asks, his voice now cracking.

"No, I would never hate him," I say to him.

"Then why didn't you let me see him?"

"I don't know..." I have no words to defend myself.

"You hate him," Alex insists and frees himself from my embrace, "leave me alone, Mom."

As he leaves me to myself, I bury my face in my hands and cry my heart out.

I need to keep my job. I can't afford to get myself fired right now, and it makes it difficult to get another job. Peak Bites being the top catering service in Malibu, if anyone finds out I was fired from Peak Bites, nobody with better opportunities will hire me.

Todd was slowly ruining my life. And I was letting him do it. He made me chase away the man I love. And now my son won't speak to me. There was no way I was going to let him have custody of Alex after this.

"What the hell happened to you?" Allison asked, "Why are there dark circles under your eyes? Were you crying? Did someone hurt you?"

I stared at her and looked around me. Some of the other staff had the same look on their faces. Anytime I came here, I always had my head held high, but I can barely lift my head to look at them today.

Besides Allison and the other staff who have been on my side, it feels like the rest of them are mocking me with their eyes.

I can't hold it back anymore, and I burst into tears.

"Hey, hey, what happened?" Allison hugs me, trying to calm me down, "It's okay, I'm here."

I know she's here for me, but she's not the only one I need a hug from right now.

I drove down to his place this morning and found it empty. His house was locked, his things were still inside, but his car was gone.

Security at the bottom of the hill told me he left yesterday, returning to New York just like I had asked him to do.

I couldn't sleep last night as I thought about what I said to him. I even told him to go back to his playboy lifestyle when all he wanted to do was to help me. I pushed him away, thinking I could handle it by myself, but in reality, I couldn't.

I tried talking to Alex earlier today, but he refused to answer me. Lily looked disappointed to see me after I told her what happened. She took Alex to her place and asked me to sort things out myself.

I have absolutely no idea what I'm doing anymore, and there's no one I can talk to for help.

"Let's go outside, okay?" Allison suggests.

"Okay," I reply weakly. Wiping my tears.

We find a spot to sit outside, and I tell her everything that happened.

"I know you had no other choice. Pushing him away was the only option you had to protect him, wasn't it?" She asks.

ARROGANT BILLIONAIRE'S DO-OVER

"I can't lose my job now. I hate this place, but I still need my job to take care of myself and Alex. This job gives me experience to start my own restaurant or catering service someday," I explain.

"Does it really have to be Peak Bites?" She asks, "Look, I know you are one of the best chefs I've ever met in Malibu. If no one wants to hire you because you got fired from a crummy place like Peak Bites, then you don't want to work there, either."

"Besides, you and I draw in more customers to this restaurant than anyone else here," she continues, "yes, getting a new job may be hard, but that doesn't mean you won't ever find a new job. I'm sure there will be restaurants that you'd love to work at. They would fight themselves just to get you on their team. That's how valuable you are. And you worked hard to make yourself that valuable. Peak Bites didn't do that for you. You did it yourself."

She pauses and continues, "You can do this, okay?"

"I just..." I pause, "I've already created the mindset that I'm able to handle things on my own. If I show this weakness..."

"The other day, you told me that Kevin asked you to teach him how to cook," she cuts me off, "Did you think that was a sign of weakness?"

"No..."

"It's the same thing. You have someone who loves you very much. At least that's what I think about his feelings for you," she continues, "Don't you think he would like you to trust him and ask him for help?"

I don't know why, but I just remembered when he helped me babysit Alex. I will never forget the image of him bonding with my son, and he looked so happy to be able to help me.

I was at a loss for what to do that day, and yet he offered to help me. Even when he had no idea what he was doing. He's always been like that.

"Besides, you're pregnant," she reminds me, "and he's still not aware that he is the father. If he truly loves you, he won't let you down."

"Do you love him?" She asks.

"With every fiber of my being," I finally admit it, "I love how grumpy he is sometimes. I love it when he gets stubborn. I love how he cares for my son like he's his. I love how he makes love to me. I love how he makes me feel safe while I work. I love how he listens to me. I love the fact that no matter how many times I push him away, he is ready to help me if I ever need it."

"I don't think you should be telling me all this," she laughs, "You know who deserves to hear it."

"You're right," I wipe my tears. I feel better already.

"There you are. I've been looking all over for you," Todd announces as he makes his way towards us.

"What are you doing here?" I glare at him.

"Is he the one who ruined everything?" Allison asks, and I nod.

"I'm glad you canceled the contract," he says while placing his hand on his chest to show his appreciation, "I'm really happy that you're considering our relationship."

"I am not considering our relationship," I say as I get to my feet, "I just realized that canceling the contract was a big mistake on my part."

"It's kind of too late for that," he says, "so when can I come see Alex? Can we split him? I have him for three days, and you have him for the remaining four days?"

"You won't get any custody of Alex," I answer, "And you won't get a relationship with me, either."

"Do you want to lose your job that badly?" He asks, "I could just go inside right now and talk to my uncle..."

"Go right ahead," I smile, "please, I insist."

The shocked expression on his face switches to one of rage.

"Say that again," he challenges me.

"Think about it, Todd," I say to him, "what kind of mother would allow a bully to be a father to her child?"

"And I'm guessing a sleazebag who sleeps around with different women and just recently had a scandal is a perfect father figure?" He smirks.

"At least he would never threaten to destroy my career if he doesn't get his way," I yell at him.

His inability to intimidate me only infuriates him further, and he retreats to the restaurant.

"Oh well, I'd better go and brush up my resume," I sigh.

"Right behind you," she says.

"Wait, why would you do that?"

She gives me a quizzical look, "so you want to get fired and leave me alone here with these losers? Nuh-uh, I'm coming with you."

"Thank you, Allison," I hug her, and she embraces me, too.

"Do you think switching the salt and sugar containers would be too much?" Allison asks.

"Don't you even dare...," I grin.

Chapter 25

Yes, I Will

Lydia

I'm out of a job.

Luckily, I have enough money saved. The last job with Kevin paid a lot, and I have some from investments. I just need to find a new job within a couple of months to make sure I can provide for all the necessities.

I still need to work on my relationship with my son. I knock on his room door and let myself in. He's reverted back into a quiet boy. No longer mischievous, just quiet. On the bed, he's reading one of the books Kevin used to read to him.

"Hey baby," I caught his attention.

"Hey, Mom," he responds and returns to his book.

I take in a deep breath and make my way to the bed, sitting by his side, "Are you still mad at me?"

"No," he replies. And I can tell he means it.

"I see."

"Mommy, why are you always at home?" He asks.

"Mommy doesn't have a job anymore," I chuckle dryly.

"No job?"

"Yes…"

"What does it mean?" He asks.

"I'm not earning any money right now, but I have some money saved so I can still take care of you, okay?" I tell him.

"Uncle Kevin told me about his job one time," as soon as he mentions Kevin's name, he seems sad, returning his thoughts to his book once more.

"Do you miss him?" I ask.

"A lot."

"I miss him a lot too," I tell him.

He asks, "Then why did you make him leave in the first place?"

"Listen to me, sweetie. I don't know how, but I'm going to make this right, okay?" I promise him.

"Okay," his face brightens up with a smile, and I feel motivated to take the next step.

"Any luck?" Allison asks.

"To be honest, I haven't started job hunting yet," I admit, "I didn't expect the news of me being fired to spread this quickly."

A news article posted the tweet of me being fired. Luckily for me, Peak Bites didn't share the reason why I was fired. But now that I think about it, they might have done that to protect themselves.

If they did any further investigation and found out the original reason why I was fired, people might stop going to the restaurant.

There really was no any good reason.

"It sucks to be you," she says, "but honestly, this might be the perfect time to go job hunting. Since people don't know why you were fired, they are curious to hear your side of the story. You could use that to your advantage."

"I really don't know how to use a situation like this to my advantage. It feels underhanded," I reply, "maybe I'll just find a small place to work. They won't ask any questions, will they?"

"From a top catering service to a small restaurant nobody heard about?" She asks, "Not that there's anything wrong with a small place, but it's a downgrade. Are you sure you want to do that?"

"Well, it could be the downgrade that leads to the next upgrade," I respond, trying to sound optimistic.

"I'll keep looking at the high-end restaurants," she says, "I'll put in a good word for you."

"Thank you, baby," I smile.

"Speaking of a baby," she says, "Have you contacted Kevin?"

"It might be too late to do that," I reply, "I honestly don't know how to face him or if he would even listen after what I did."

"Well, there's only one way to find out," she says, "Call him and ask him directly."

"I'll try my best," I assure her.

Two Weeks Later

I haven't been able to get a job. Nobody wants to hire me because they are suspicious of my reasons for being fired.

Even when I tried to tell them what happened, they did not believe me.

At this point, I've given up. I can't cash in some of my investments for another month. My sister has been helping me financially temporarily.

There's nothing I can do.

ARROGANT BILLIONAIRE'S DO-OVER

Allison has been able to get a job, but even as she puts in a good word for me, they still don't want to hire me.

The only way out of this is to start my own business and change the narrative for myself. But I need some capital to start with.

I'll start with cooking food at home and delivering it to my clients.

"And Kevin Wills has once again proven that you don't have to be in Hollywood to make a name for yourself," the news anchor reports, "just a few months ago, he was faced with a scandal. And now both he and Sandra were seen on the sets of the new movie project. This man has no enemies. This movie project is the biggest of its time, and a lot of agencies have been going after it, but Kevin has proven to be the one who gets what he wants."

Kevin is enjoying a good life, and at this point, I feel he's already forgotten about me and Alex.

It hurts because I was the one who chased him away. If there's anything I can do to fix my relationship with him, I would do it. I just want to apologize to him. I want to tell him how sorry I am for everything I did.

The sound of the doorbell interrupts my thoughts.

"Lilly is late today," I remark as I go to answer it.

I open the door and I find a handsome man, arrogant and yet the kindest person I know, standing in front of my door, holding a bouquet of roses in his hand and looking nervous.

"Kevin?" I can barely believe my eyes.

"Sorry it took so long," he replies.

I jump into his arms, causing him to drop the flowers in order to accept my hug.

"Oh my God, Kevin, Kevin," I repeatedly call his name.

"I'm here," he assures me, "I'm not going anywhere. Not anymore."

"I'm sorry I chased you away," I start to apologize, "You asked me over and over again to open up to you, and I refused. I was stubborn, thinking I could handle it by myself."

"It's okay," he says softly.

"No, it's not okay," I hit his chest weakly, "I still ended up losing everything. My job, my relationship with Alex, and you."

"The only thing you lost was your job," he says, "there's nothing like you losing me or Alex. We're both here for you."

I'm holding back the urge to cry.

"There's something I have to tell you," his gaze softens, "I've been keeping something secret from you."

"What?" I ask.

"When I found out you were going to be my chef, I was ready to have you replaced," he replies.

"Well, that makes two of us," I grin.

"I would have sworn you were excited to work for me," he teases.

"You paid well," I shrug.

We both chuckle softly.

"You made me realize that I had been going through my life all wrong," he continues, "Before I knew it, I wanted a life with you and Alex by my side. I'm sorry it took me so long to finally say it, but I have hopelessly fallen in love with you."

"I thought you would forget about me," I say to him, "because of what I did."

"You're too deep in my mind to be forgotten," he assures me. Then, he searches his pocket for something and shows me the ring box, "Will you give me the honor of eating your meals every day for the rest of my life in exchange for my undying love and devotion?"

"Wait... before that," I stop him, "There's something I've been keeping from you as a secret, and you need to know."

"Well, there are two things actually," I explain nervously, "One, I kept my feelings hidden from you because I was scared you'd hurt me again. To be honest, I'm still scared, but I want to believe that you won't."

"You have nothing to worry about my love for you," he assures me, "what's the second secret?"

"I'm... I'm pregnant," I answer.

His eyes widen in disbelief, "Wait, what? You're joking, right?"

Oh no...He doesn't want the baby...

"I'm being honest," I respond.

"Mine?" He asks, his eyes gleaming.

"Yes, of course, the baby is yours," I answer, "I'm almost ten weeks..."

He gets to his feet, holds me tight, and kisses me deeper than ever.

As he pulls away, he's beaming with joy, "Will you marry me, Lydia? You have to say yes!"

"Yes! Of course, yes! I didn't expect you to be this happy," I admit.

"Why wouldn't I be happy?" He asks, "Does Alex know he's going to be a big brother?"

"Not yet," I reply.

"Uncle Kevin?!" Alex yells as he runs past me and embraces Kevin, "I missed you so much."

"I missed you a lot more," Kevin says as he squeezes the little boy.

Once again, he's warmed my heart.

"Kevin?" I call.

"Yes?" He answers.

"I will marry you."

Chapter 26

Our Future

Kevin

After returning to Malibu, I originally planned to help her start a business first, but instead, I asked her to marry me.

I was overwhelmed with joy when she told me she was pregnant. I couldn't sleep well from the excitement, and heck, I still can't. Thinking about becoming a father still delights me.

Here's what happened after the proposal.

"I will marry you," she answered.

"I will never let you down as your husband," I promised her.

"Do you want to come in?" She asked.

"Sure, thanks."

I got comfortable on the sofa. Alex refused to let me go, and I didn't want to let him go either.

It had only been a few weeks, but it felt longer. I had deviated from my original plan, so it was time to get back on track.

"I saw the tweets," I said, "You were let go from Peak Bites. Do you think you can finally tell me why it happened?"

"I had to push you away because of Todd," she replied, "Todd was my ex and Alex's biological father."

I had to take another look at Alex because he didn't look anything like his father.

"I think I can already guess what's on your mind," she chuckled.

"And I'm glad he didn't take any traits from him," I added.

"Anyway," she continued, "Todd wanted custody of Alex and a second chance to be with me. When I refused him, he threatened to get me fired. That was when I found out his uncle owned Peak Pites. His uncle had already been looking for an opportunity to get rid of me because he didn't care for my popularity among his clients. Revealing my relationship with you was the perfect leverage he could use to blackmail me."

As she explained what happened, it only angered me. I couldn't believe something like that happened.

ARROGANT BILLIONAIRE'S DO-OVER

Because James hired a private investigator and ran background information, I knew Todd had an uncle who owned Peak Bites.

"Have you been able to get another job?" I asked.

"No one seems interested in my side of the story," she responded.

"I'm sorry. In a way, this is my fault," I apologized, "because of our relationship, you lost your job."

"That's okay. It was my choice to leave that job, but I want to ask you for a favor. I'm wondering if you could help me." She said.

"That's new..."

"I need a loan. I'll start my own business, and I'll pay you back," she said.

"What do you have in mind as your own business? Catering service?" I asked.

"Yes, but picture something like what I did for you," she started to explain, "I want to create an opportunity where people could order or subscribe to a full meal plan consisting of breakfast, dinner, and lunch."

"So basically, you prepare the food for them and deliver it?" I ask, "but not necessarily takeouts."

"Yes, especially for the families with members who don't know how to cook or are too busy to cook," she added.

"Got it. How much do you need?" I asked, "And don't think of paying me back. By the way, I came here to help you with your business today.

I haven't planned on proposing yet, but you look so beautiful, and I was so happy to see you that I didn't want to wait until your business was up and running before I could propose. Plus, I felt if I wasted any more time, someone else would snatch you."

"And here I was thinking you came all this way to propose to me," she laughed, "But thank you for making sure no one snatches me."

After that, we got to work.

We were able to partner with Mr. Roger Henry to give her the kitchen space she needed.

While I wanted to give her everything she wanted, the woman I have fallen in love with insisted she does things her own way.

My role is to watch from the sidelines and cheer her on.

It took a while, with the growing pregnancy, to get things to where she wanted it to be.

By the fifth month of her pregnancy, she was able to bring in many customers for her new business.

Even the mayor became a patron even though he understood she wouldn't be his personal chef.

I was so proud of her. What she had accomplished in such a short time while she was pregnant was amazing.

We got married around the same time, and she wasn't shy about rocking her wedding gown with her growing belly.

She looked so beautiful that I had to beg her to let me have multiple weddings with her.

One regular wedding at the church.

Another at the beach.

And one right here at my property on the hill.

It was known as the wedding of the century.

I slowly open my eyes and turn to my side. She's still asleep, and her soft breathing is like therapy to me. I brush aside two strands of hair covering her face and rest my hands on her cheek.

She slowly opens her eyes and stares at me, a confused expression on her face. She's still half-asleep, but I can tell what comes next.

She moves closer to my face and kisses my lips softly. Then she wakes up and realizes what she's done.

"Good morning," she greets, her ears red as a tomato.

"Good morning to you too, sleepyhead," I reply, "Had a wonderful dream."

"I'm still in it," she says as she covers her face with both hands.

"Should I wake you up?" I get on top of her, being cautious of her belly. She's almost seven months pregnant now.

She nods bashfully.

The pregnancy hormones have her acting a lot more bashful than usual. I kiss the hands covering her face repeatedly until she finally removes them from her face. I kiss her lips gently, just the way she likes it.

She whimpers under my mouth and sticks her tongue into my mouth hesitantly. As I start to suck on her tongue, she tries to pull it back in, but I don't let her escape.

She moans in protest until she finally gives in to the pleasure, opening her mouth to get more of her tongue in my mouth.

I stop the kiss and focus on her darkened areola. Her nipples have also gotten bigger in size, anticipating the burdens of motherhood that are yet to come.

I nibble the undersides of her right breast, where she's more sensitive, and her body jerks in response. Then I return my mouth to trap her nipples between my teeth.

I don't bite down with full force as her breasts have gotten softer, making her very sensitive to pain.

Just flicking against her clit, is enough to make her cling to the sheets in glorious pleasure.

She's adopted the habit of falling asleep while naked or barely clothed. Lucky for me, it's the former today.

I keep my head between her legs and kiss her pussy. The string of her wetness, connecting my lips to her entrance is visible.

"Hurry..." she demands as I spread her pussy open. Her wetness makes it look like I'm parting the pink sea. I kiss her entire pussy, before eating her out.

"Oh... Kevin...," she calls out for me.

"Shh... don't wake up Alex," I warn as I rub her pussy with my fingers, applying pressure to her clit while she slowly moves her hips to match my pace.

As I slid two fingers inside while my thumb continues to massage her clit, she arches her back and bite her lips to avoid making loud moans.

"Baby... I'm done with fingers...," she pleads, "I want him inside," she grabs my dick.

"Please..." she begs.

"All right, as you wish," I respond as I put my throbbing dick on her pussy and start rubbing it against her on the surface until I finally slide into her.

I use only half of my length at first to make sure I won't hurt her.

It feels like a tight ravine inside of her.

As I move, she throws her head back in pleasure.

The sound against her pussy as I move in and out seems to only increase with her wetness.

I grab her breasts for support, and she continues to moan, maintaining eye contact as I bring her closer to the edge.

I pull out and have her bend over, raising her ass to me.

I can go deeper, and this time, I allow her to handle the movements on her own.

With each loving thrust, I can feel she's about to climax, judging by how she increases her pace.

"Easy baby," I tell her, "You don't have to rush. Just take your time and enjoy me, okay?"

"Okay... Aww..."

"That's my girl," I praise as I take over, moving with a more precise rhythm and deeper thrusts to make her get to her destination faster.

As we climax, I collapse next to her, both of us catching our breaths.

"I'm so glad we met again," I say to her, "In fact, I'm thankful that the scandal happened because it gave me the chance to reconnect with the love of my life."

"And I'm glad we met again," she agrees.

"I love you, my stubborn chef."

"I love you, my arrogant playboy."

We kiss each other again, chuckling at the nicknames.

Epilogue

Lydia

Five Years Later

Kevin has managed to remain at the top of the game through his talent agency and plans to retire early so that he can spend more time with us.

As for me, my catering service has become one of the biggest in Malibu.

Peak Bites struggled to remain afloat after Allison and I left. So, with the money I made from my catering business, I bought Peak Bites.

Allison now handles Peak Bites, and it's turned into a success once again.

Todd asked me for forgiveness, and I finally did forgive him. He got to see Alex once or twice, but eventually, he moved on with his life and got married. I haven't seen him for a few years, but the last time I checked, he was doing okay.

"Dad, we're going to be late!" Alex yells as he gets ready to leave for school.

"I'm almost done packing!' Kevin replied as he put a boiled egg in his lunch box.

"Daddy, I want extra sausage," Ruth demanded – she's our five-year-old daughter, an exact female replica of her father.

"Oh geez, fine," Kevin agrees and places the extra sausage.

The sound of a car honking outside hastens the chaos.

"Auntie Lily is going to leave us," Alex reports.

"Lunch is done!" He announces and finishes putting the food in their lunch boxes.

My sister got a remote job opportunity for tech support and volunteers to take the kids to elementary school and kindergarten.

I kiss my babies goodbye and watch them make their way to the car where she's parked.

"Phew... I'm glad that's out of the way," Kevin let out a sigh of relief. Then turns to me, "How did I do?"

"You know, when you said you'd be handling the lunch, I didn't expect it would be this chaotic," I answer and kiss his cheek, "A for the entertainment."

"That's my job baby," he says as he kisses my lips, "Now let's get ready to see Allison and her new baby."

Yes, you heard that right. After many years of trying, Allison and her husband finally welcomed their baby last night. Both the mom and the baby are doing well.

Everyone's life seems to be falling into place, and my life can't be any better.

I had given up on finding the right man. I never expected that Kevin would be someone I could get along with.

But now, I have a happy family with him.

"What are you staring at me for?" Kevin asks with a raised brow, "Sorry, ma'am, I'm a married man."

"Yes, my handsome married man," I agree as I take off my shirt.

"No, no, we're going to be late," he protests but barely resisting.

And that's the story of an arrogant playboy turned husband.

THE END

If you enjoy this book, check out Next Door Billionaire's Surprise Baby, https://www.amazon.com/dp/B0CQ5G4GGand Silver fox Daddy's Baby Secret Box Set: https://www.amazon.com/dp/B0CND36HFP

Also By

Next Door Billionaire's Surprise Baby: https://www.amazon.com/dp/B0CRZ59BX1

Also By

Silver Fox Daddy's Baby Secret Box Set:: https://www.amazon.com/dp/B0CND36HFP

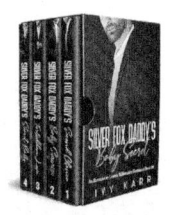

Also By

Billionaire Grump's Secret Love: https://www.amazon.com/dp/B0C7CPQS47

ALSO BY

Do you like FREEBIE Romance Books?

Sign Up For My Newsletters and

Get Billionaire Boss's Secret Baby for FREE!

https://dl.bookfunnel.com/9hnfoy43gx

Printed in Great Britain
by Amazon